MORE MYSTERY BY KRISTINE KATHRYN RUSCH

ALSO BY KRISTINE KATHRYN RUSCH

THE FEY SERIES

MORE FROM THE FEY

Destiny: A Story of The Fey

Lessons From The Writing of The Fey

THE FATES UNIVERSE

WRITING AS KRISTINE GRAYSON

The Charming Trilogy, Vol. 1

The Charming Trilogy, Vol. 2

The Fates Trilogy

The Daughters of Zeus Trilogy

KIZZIE

A RUSCH CRIME STORY

KRISTINE KATHRYN RUSCH

KIZZIE

KIZZIE

Kizzie called Mike from school.

He was in his Porsche, heading to the office late because he had put in what felt like a thousand hours the day before. The case had been a small one until it blew up, like cases sometimes did.

He took the call at a stoplight in the center of town because he always answered Kizzie's calls as close to the first ring as possible.

"Uncle Mike," she said, "Daddy's at the school. I just saw him pull up."

The comment—and the fear in Kizzie's voice—sent a responding jolt of fear through Mike. He made a U-turn the moment the light changed, ignoring all the cars that were coming toward him, and headed toward the Braunland Educational Complex, hoping he could get there fast enough.

Kizzie's father was Mike's old fraternity brother, Luke Brocato. Luke had become someone unrecognizable in the past ten years. He had gone from a rather loud party animal to a ferocious attorney to simply ferocious.

Mike Cummings had gone along for part of the ride—inseparable in college, later separated by law school itself as Luke partied more than he studied, then best man at the wedding gone wrong, and ultimately a named party in the divorce from hell, a divorce that, if one looked closely at the evidence, he had nothing to do with.

Initially, Mike had nothing legally to do with Kizzie either, although at her birth, he had been chosen as her godfather. Luke had laughed at the name. *Makes you sound like a Mafia guy*, Luke had said with a big grin, because they both knew that, of the two of them, Mike was the one who never broke the rules, particularly after he passed the bar.

Stop, Luke, Mike would say whenever Luke tried to do something shady. *We're officers of the court. We can't do that crap anymore.*

As if Mike had wanted to do that crap before. He had never taken part in Luke's schemes. That had been Luke's biological brother, Gary, a man who seemed to have no boundaries at all.

Mike looked at it all askance, even when he was in pre-law. He discovered early on that he loved the law more than he loved any single human being. Because of this, he never married. Girlfriends would get tired of his ceaseless study and willingness to dig deep into the most arcane corners of the law, looking for insight.

You shoulda been a professor, Luke had said during one of their legal discussions just after law school. But Mike hadn't wanted a professorship. He wanted a judgeship, most particularly on the court of appeals. And he wanted to be appointed. He didn't want to work his way up, going through election after election while he served in places like family court.

Family court, where, it was said, the best people were on their worst behavior.

Hell, buddy, Luke said after Mike had said something about that, *that's why I work criminal law. The worst people on their best behavior.*

It seemed so simple then, before Amanda, before Kizzie, before the night of Kizzie's birth when Luke had been too drunk to drive and passed out in the waiting room. He hadn't even made it to the birthing suite.

It had been Mike who took Kizzie, newly swaddled, from the nurse and handed her to Amanda, Mike who had learned all the Lamaze breathing and coaching techniques to help his own sister and got to use them a second time while Amanda struggled with labor. Mike, who had looked down at Kizzie's unfocused blue eyes and little perfect bow of a mouth, saw the abundant black curls that most newborns did not have, felt the whisper of little fingers on his own gigantic thumb, and fell deeply, fully, and completely in love.

Kizzie was his girl from that day, and she knew it. She preferred him to Luke. She would stop crying when Mike was around. She would fall asleep on his shoulder, let him feed her when she got fussy, giggled when he scooped her off the floor and swung her around, her little feet encased in footie pajamas extended out wide.

It was Mike she called when Mom and Dad fought, Mike who would take her to pizza or his place while the warring couple supposedly settled their differences, and Mike who gave Kizzie and Amanda a home for the first month when Luke fought the divorce so hard that Amanda had no income at all.

Mike wasn't in love with Amanda. He'd never really liked her much, but he cared for her, the way a person cared for a sibling whose personality grated.

But oh, that Kizzie. She was his, the child he never had. The child he wished he could have.

He never told anyone that, but Kizzie understood.

Which was why, at the age of eleven, voice thick with tears, she had called him and said, "Daddy's here, and he shouldn't be."

D amn straight he shouldn't have been. Luke had lost the right to unsupervised custody the day he slapped Amanda across the mouth in the hallway of the Ernest A. Fidelio Justice Center just before yet another divorce hearing. She didn't have to fake her response—the blood, the broken tooth, the bruising that started the moment Luke's hand left her skin. He had done real damage, the kind that got a man in serious trouble when he did it outside of a courthouse.

Inside, the trouble doubled. Then doubled again because Luke was an officer of the court.

He was arrested for assault, Amanda was whisked off to the hospital, and Mike was the one who picked up Kizzie that day from school. Only nine at that point, and even then, she knew something awful was going on.

Uncle Mike, she had said, *can I just live with you?*

Yeah, him. The single, unmarried guy who hung around because he liked the kid. That wasn't suspicious at all—at least not from a legal and law enforcement point of view.

The authorities didn't know the background, the history, the look in those unfocused blue eyes the day she was born, eyes that eventually turned a smart and savvy brown, with an intelligence so far off the charts that it had to be nurtured.

He tried not to hate her parents who were more concerned with their own crap than they were with the brilliant daughter they were forgetting to raise.

He understood what it was like to live Kizzie's life, even though he never told her that. His warring parents had done the same thing with him and his little sister, ignoring them for the joys of domestic war. But at least he'd had a sibling who understood, who gave him someone to talk to, and who escaped with him the moment they figured out how to get their asses out of that house.

Kizzie had no one.

Luke's parents were still married, but only because alcohol-induced stupors made even the most unpleasant relationship bearable. Amanda's parents lived in Florida and visited once a year, seeing Amanda and Kizzie on their best behavior.

Who the hell wants to be around those judgmental pricks? Luke would say from the beginning of that marriage, and so he never really developed a relationship with them, and Amanda never told them the worst of what she suffered under Luke's temper.

Amanda's sisters tried, but they were wrapped up in their own lives around the country, lives Mike never learned much about. One sister, Georgina, tried to fund an escape for both Amanda and Kizzie, but to do that, Amanda would have had to give up everything she'd worked for here and move to North Dakota.

It had been a good offer, and one Mike wanted Amanda to take. Georgina and her husband Karl were good people, with three girls of their own. They lived in Fargo, and he'd checked—it had a great school system.

Moving there would have been best for Kizzie, but

Amanda never thought about what was best for Kizzie. To Amanda, Kizzie was a burden, someone to drag through Amanda's drama, and somehow was expected to survive it.

Mike suspected Kizzie was smart enough to have survived it on her own, but she managed to survive it better because he was at her side.

Uncle Mike, who knew the best ice cream shops. Uncle Mike, who let her cry on his shoulder. Uncle Mike, the only one with time to help on the homework. Uncle Mike, who had two guest rooms, one of which had slowly evolved into Kizzie's home away from home—especially in the middle of some very dark nights before the divorce, when the screaming and the slapping and the hitting sometimes devolved into broken dishes and tossed furniture.

No one said anything about Mike's involvement in Kizzie's life until Luke's brother, Gary, became Luke's divorce attorney. Gary was the kind of jerk lawyer who didn't want to do the work; he'd rather cast aspersions and hint at malfeasance, something that worked with a handful of judges in the county.

The rest hated seeing Gary walk into the courtroom, because they knew he'd file too many motions, pump up his bill, and do the minimum for his client—even when his client was his only brother.

All Gary's arrival on the scene did was show how far Luke had fallen. Once, he could have afforded the best divorce attorney in the county. Now, he could barely afford his incompetent brother.

Amanda did have the best divorce attorney in the county, but only because Mike paid for her. Mike didn't want Amanda to lose custody of Kizzie because of aspersions or an imbalance in the proceedings or because of some technicality.

What he really wanted was for Amanda to escape this entire town with her daughter, but so far, Amanda had fought that, even though Georgina's North Dakota offer remained on the table.

The one thing—the only thing—Mike had managed to do was to get Amanda to write her will. Her divorce attorney, Serena Tomlinson, had helped him convince Amanda, saying, *Without one, if something happens to you, she goes to Luke no matter what.*

That had scared Amanda enough to complete her will that very week, and she told Mike she had done that.

Something happens to me, she had said, *you make sure that will gets to court, before Luke tries anything.*

Mike promised, just like he had promised so many other things.

Sometimes he felt like he was the only responsible one in the relationship…and it wasn't even his relationship.

Except with Kizzie. He wasn't ever going to give up on Kizzie.

Three days before Kizzie's school phone call, Mike bitched about Amanda and Luke to his friend Jasper over beers at their favorite watering hole. Mike could confide in Jasper. Jasper was a forensic psychologist who knew

Amanda and Luke slightly. Jasper had analyzed more divorcing couples for court than he could count.

When Mike bitched, Jasper usually just shook his head. In this instance, though, Jasper leaned back, folded his meaty hands over his stomach, and launched into his professorial mode.

Divorcing couples fall into a handful of categories, Jasper said with deliberate precision, the kind professors used for information-heavy lectures. *The first category doesn't need me. They want to get rid of each other, so they do a quickie divorce, divide the assets, and move on.*

Mike frowned. That wasn't Amanda and Luke...or anyone else he knew.

I bet that's rare, he said.

I don't know if it's rare, Jasper said, sounding slightly annoyed at being interrupted. *I never see those folks. The others—well, if the divorce takes longer than a few months, then they're still wrapped up in each other.*

That described Amanda and Luke perfectly. Both of them wanted to discuss the other over and above anything new in their lives. Mike hated it and sometimes thought that the main reason Amanda didn't want to leave town was because she didn't want to stop fighting with Luke.

Usually, Jasper had continued, clearly seeing that he had Mike's attention, *the couple is still bound by strong emotion, only now that emotion is hatred.*

That fit. Mike had sighed and shaken his head. If not for Kizzie, he would walk away from all of this.

Sometimes, though, Jasper had said, *they are caught up in a game. The game usually involves one-upmanship and the desire to win at all costs.*

Mike had looked at him sharply. *Is that what you think is happening here?* he had asked.

That was when Jasper had sat up, professorial mode gone. *I hope not,* he had said. *Because those entanglements never end well.*

Mike shivered. *What do you mean?*

I mean, Jasper said, *in some of these cases, the goal is complete annihilation of the other.*

Mike's mouth had gone dry. *Do you mean murder?*

Usually that's too simple, Jasper had said. *Usually it's a combination of financial, mental, and emotional annihilations. If you kill the other, then the game vanishes too.*

Mike had struggled to understand that. *So the game is the important thing?*

Yeah, Jasper had said and looked pointedly at him.

Jasper often looked pointedly at Mike when Mike was being obtuse. Mike was missing something; something important.

You're warning me, aren't you? Mike asked, knowing he had missed a subtlety. Why couldn't Jasper speak plainly? People were often elliptical, and Mike hated that. That was why he preferred research and the law library to clients and court. Research and the law were open to interpretation, but they were never elliptical.

People who play games, Jasper had said, *often divorce, but they don't stop fighting. Everyone around them gets roped in.*

Even Kizzie, Mike had said.

Especially Kizzie, Jasper had said. *Kizzie is the prize.*

Mike literally bent over his beer, cupping the glass in his hands. The glass was cool but was warming under his touch. He no longer wanted a drink. His stomach churned, and he cursed himself for not seeing this.

When Jasper pointed it out, it seemed so obvious. This felt like one of those moments in a first-year law school class where the professor presented a conundrum, had students discuss it, and then, when they had missed the point, explained it himself.

It always felt like this, always felt like scales were lifted from Mike's eyes, in the Biblical manner, anyway, and he could see clearly.

There was no escape for Kizzie, no final divorce, no end to the fighting, not without some kind of intervention.

Clearly, Georgina and her husband Karl knew that or sensed it, which was why they kept their offer on the table.

If only Mike was more of a people-person. If only he knew how to slowly change a person's mind, to get that person to come around.

What do we do? he asked Jasper.

Jasper had given him a sad, lost smile. *There's nothing we can do, Mike. They're adults, and Kizzie is their child. She's subject to their choices. We have no legal way to intervene.*

Mike had pushed his beer glass away. *You deal with these kinds of things all the time, don't you?*

Sadly, yes, Jasper had said, taking a sip of his beer.

How do you do it? Mike asked.

I don't love them, Jasper said. *They're my clients. I stay as emotionally uninvolved as possible.*

What do I do? Mike asked.

Nothing, Jasper said. *Absolutely nothing.*

Mike did not accept nothing. He *could* not accept nothing. Nothing meant that Kizzie's life was always going to be hell, and she might even become part of an annihilation scenario, whatever that meant.

He couldn't allow that.

He knew how to stop a game. It was simple. You walked away.

He would have walked away if he were on his own. He didn't need to see friends annihilate each other, whatever that meant.

But he wasn't on his own. And Kizzie couldn't walk away.

So, he had to figure something out. He needed his big, gigantic brain to come up with a solution.

And for him, solutions always started with research— the kind of research he was deep in the middle of when Kizzie called for help.

The Harry S. Braunlund Elementary School was part of the Braunlund Educational Complex that stood on top of a ridge in the center of town. The Educational Complex included a middle school (named after Harry S.'s wife, Martha E.) and a high school (named after Harry S.'s father, Harold Raymund).

The Complex was surrounded by parking lots and athletic fields. There were no other buildings nearby. The closest neighborhood was halfway down the hill and went off into the distance.

The Complex had been designed in the 1970s with only one major road in and one major road out. Locals knew to avoid that road at 7 a.m and 3 p.m, when it was filled with buses and cars from the high school kids privileged enough to drive their own.

Twice a day, elementary school parents lined the parking lot in front of the Harry S. school. The young parents—the ones whose oldest (or only) child was in their first year at Harry S.—often stood outside their vehicles nervously awaiting or dropping off their child.

There were private schools in the city that were among the best in the state, but Amanda hadn't been able to afford the tuition, and Luke had said repeatedly from the moment Kizzie approached school age, *Why the hell would we pay for a school when there are perfectly good free ones around here?*

On that, he wasn't wrong. The idea behind the Education Complex had been simple: consolidate all of the city's public schools into a central location, hire the best teachers, and free up the kids to learn.

That the consolidation also stopped court-mandated bussing during the Civil Rights Era wasn't mentioned, nor was the fact that the Braunlund family got all kinds of massive continuing perks from the state government for donating the land and the initial building costs to the city.

Still, sending Kizzie to the Complex had been one of the few things about her childhood that Mike had agreed with Luke on. Otherwise, Mike would have put up the tuition—and he considered it. But he researched the private schools and found that they actually lacked a lot of the amenities built into the Complex.

He hadn't really thought about the Complex and the fact that it had been a *choice* until that morning, as he sped up the hill, cursing himself for not getting Kizzie into a smaller school, one with a lot of security and a snobbishly closed campus.

The campus at the Complex was terrifyingly open, designed in a day when no one thought about mass school shootings or bombing schools that *children* attended—although someone should have thought of it, given all the bombings that had gone on at universities all over the country as the Complex had been planned.

As he drove, all Mike could think about were the doors everywhere on the Harry S. building. Because the building sprawled across nearly three blocks, there were at least two mandated exits in each wing—often more. He knew that the state fire code meant that the windows—of which there were also a bunch—could serve as exits as well, but that was in case of fire, which was all anyone thought about when this damn building was built.

No one thought about keeping people *out*, just about how people inside could escape should the situation become dire.

As he drove to the school, he tried to call Amanda's attorney but was told she was in the middle of a deposition and unavailable. He told the legal secretary that Luke was at the school and was not allowed there. He knew the legal secretary well enough that she would deliver a note into the deposition, but the note might not be enough. It might be too late. It might not be urgent enough.

So, as he winged his stupidly expensive Porsche, which he had bought on a whim after landing his first big job, toward the ridge, he was glad for the horsepower but wishing he could somehow levitate himself up there.

The Porsche was too old for good Bluetooth connectivity to his phone, so he had the phone in a cradle on the center console between the seats. He had the phone dial the principal's office, and demanded to talk to Principal Hallenback herself, even though Mike had no real standing, and told her that Luke was somewhere on the property and there was an order to keep him away from Kizzie. Mike also reminded Principal Hallenback that there was a restraining order against Luke, and that the family would take serious action if Kizzie's father was allowed to take her off school grounds.

Principal Hallenback promised that she would have security beside Kizzie at all times—which Kizzie was going to complain about later, because what kid wanted her friends to know about all of her problems?—but Mike accepted that as a solution.

The principal had run this drill before, with other parents. She also knew that Mike was listed as a secondary contact if Amanda couldn't be reached. Mike was cleared to pick Kizzie up from school or to act in Amanda's stead.

Luke wasn't supposed to get near his daughter on campus at all.

Mike was halfway up the hill when Principal Hallenback called back.

"We can't find her," Principal Hallenback said. "But we do have eyes on Mr. Brocato. She is not with him. In fact, he's waiting in my outer office because my secretary has told him that she will see what she can do to bring Kizzie to him."

"What?" Mike asked. He wasn't sure which event his *what?* applied to—the fact that Kizzie couldn't be found, or that someone had promised to give Kizzie over to Luke.

"Don't worry," the principal said. "My secretary is lying for me. I'm not at the office. I'm helping security find Kizzie."

Mike hung up without saying goodbye. He had the phone redial Kizzie.

"Where are you?" he asked.

"Bathroom," she said, her voice still thick. She was in tears. "He can't come into a girl's room, right?"

Sometimes he forgot how young she actually was, not to mention the fact that, in some ways, she was more his child than anyone else's. He remembered what it was like to be ten and wonder why people did not follow the carefully crafted rules of each situation. In her mind, boys were not allowed in the girls' bathroom, ergo her dad wouldn't look for her in one.

Mike wasn't going to explain that to her, not now, not yet. "I'll be right there," he said. "I'm almost to the school now."

"Hurry," Kizzie said. "I don't want to see him."

Me either, Mike thought, but didn't say. Instead, he said, "I know, sweetie. We'll keep him from you."

As if that was a promise Mike could keep. Too much depended on other people. But he didn't say that. Instead, he made her tell him which bathroom she was in, and redialed the principal, letting her know and warning her not to have security go inside that bathroom. It would scare Kizzie too much.

He wanted to keep the poor girl as calm as possible.

He needed to keep *himself* as calm as possible, but his heart wasn't listening. He kept hearing Jasper's voice, repeating the word *annihilate.* Mike had no idea why Luke would show up at the school when he knew he was forbidden to get near it, and knew that it would impact his assault charge and maybe even get his bail rescinded.

Mike had been on edge since that conversation with Jasper, and this event—whatever the hell it was—had amplified the feeling into something akin to panic.

As he got to the Complex, he saw only a handful of cars in the various parking lots, with the most in the high school lot nearly a quarter of a mile away. Only the teachers' cars were in the elementary school lot. There didn't appear to be any parental vehicles at all, which surprised Mike.

He had thought he would see Luke's P.O.S., the car he ended up with as the work dried up for a volatile attorney who was fighting a charge of aggravated assault. The POS was a sedan with a half-finished paint job, and a dent in the back bumper. The tires were bald, and there was a crack in the windshield.

There was no way to mistake any other car for the POS.

The fact that Luke hadn't parked out front really bothered Mike. Something crawled and itched at the back of his mind. Luke had to be alone, right? He no longer had friends to help him.

Unless Gary was here too.

Mike shivered.

Maybe Luke had simply parked around the back, where no one could see him, so he wouldn't have been prevented from entering the building. There was a narrow parking strip back there, and since Kizzie had called, she had probably seen, through one of the large classroom windows, Luke pull up and park.

Luke wouldn't have done that to steal her away, unless he really had lost his mind. The school had security cameras everywhere. Luke had to know that if he tried to sneak Kizzie out of the building, the police would have arrived quickly. Luke's POS didn't have the horsepower to outrun them, even if he thought that was a good idea.

But the idea of Luke parking in the back of the building bothered Mike a lot. The classrooms on the back had the biggest windows, because they overlooked a veritable forest—the rest of the Braunlund land that hadn't been donated to the Complex.

Kids could—and did—get lost inside of that forest. There were trails—if the narrow paths that went through the trees could be called trails—and someone with knowledge of those trails could get over the ridgeline fairly easily.

Luke knew the ridgeline and the trails. Heck, so did Mike. Both men had gone to school at the Complex, and they knew the ins and outs the way any kid who had attended public school in the city knew about the various hideaways in the area.

That thought did not reassure Mike.

He didn't go around back, though. He squealed his Porsche to a stop near the front door of Harry S., and got out, almost forgetting to lock the damn car. He was so inside his head that he didn't immediately think of the usual precautions that he took here.

Kids stole cars that were unlocked, particularly the cars that looked like they were worth stealing. His Porsche was worth stealing because of its sports car status, even though it wasn't worth as much as the ugly boxy cars the teachers drove. And his Porsche was old enough that any kid with a modicum of hotwiring skills could take that car with just a few minutes of effort.

He locked the car, thought for a moment about pretending to be calm, and then decided *the hell with that* because he wasn't calm, not at all.

He jumped the curb and ran toward the school. He launched himself into the big entry, four doors across, all glass, and stepped into the so-called airlock between this and another round of doors.

The smell of dry air and gym socks greeted him, along with the faint odor of peanut butter. Normally, the smells would have made him smile, but they didn't right now. He needed to get to Kizzie. He didn't know what he was going to do with her, but he was going to have to do something.

That would problem would rise to the top of the list once he knew she was safe. One step at a time; that would be the only way to get through this morning.

Kizzie had told him that she was in the girls' bathroom on the second floor near the center of the school. He took the stairs leading up to that bathroom two at a time, even though his legs protested.

Running like this didn't help his heart, and he didn't like the way his belly fat jiggled as he moved. He wasn't that overweight—maybe twenty pounds—but he was more out of shape than he had ever been in his life.

A person didn't think about how much being in shape mattered until they were in a situation like this. He had always thought he could power through, but now he was getting to the point where powering through wasn't even a damn option.

He had no idea how he had gotten here. How any of them had gotten here. Kizzie crying in a bathroom, afraid of her father for god's sake. Mike unable to reach her mother who was not making any sensible moves in her divorce, not any more.

And that word *annihilate*. Damn Jasper for even bringing it up.

Classes were in session, and the school had that studious hush that all schools had when the kids weren't in the hallway. Mike checked his watch: it was only 10 a.m. although it felt ever-so-much later to him. Morning recess didn't start until 10:30, and then it went by grade, starting with the youngest. The oldest kids—the group Kizzie belonged to—no longer got a recess, just a really long lunch.

So he had a little time to get her out of here if he needed to before kids flooded the hallway.

The hallway seemed vast and out of proportion. The water fountains and lockers were all short, built for little kids. There were a few chairs outside of doors, as if someone had placed them there for the hall monitor, and even those chairs were too small.

The rest of the hallway was extra wide with high ceilings. The combination of the small lockers and the high ceilings made this part of the building seem even bigger than it was.

He passed room after room after room, all of them filled with kids at desks, looking straight ahead or heads bent over something. He didn't see anyone in the hall or anyone who seemed out of place.

Until he rounded the half corner to the center stairwell area. There was a wide area here, where kids sometimes congregated. The largest bathrooms on this floor were against the wall in the back. There were three—a boy's room, a girl's room, and a single-stall bathroom that had been modified for handicap access.

One of the school security guards, a burly man with black hair and a well-trimmed beard, stood in front of the girl's room, arms crossed. Mike recognized him. The guard manned the entrance in the mornings, along with a colleague, and the kids liked him. They called him by name and teased him and weren't afraid of him at all.

Which, Mike was once told, was necessary for guards at an elementary school. They had to be tough enough to scare "the bad guys" whatever that meant but gentle enough to comfort the tiniest student on their very first day.

"Principal Hallenbeck is in there," the guard said when he saw Mike.

"And Kizzie?" Mike asked.

"Yeah," the guard said.

Mike was going to ask how he knew, and then he heard the ever-so-faint voices. A woman's voice, soothing and calm, and a child's voice—Kizzie's voice—hiccoughing in panic.

"What about Luke?" Mike asked.

"I haven't seen Mr. Brocato," the guard said. "Last I heard, he was in the principal's office."

Mike nodded, and walked around the guard. The guard shifted slightly so that he could see Mike and the hallway.

Mike gently wrapped on the exterior door, and the voices stopped.

"It's Mike Cummings," he said.

"Uncle Mike!" Kizzie said, her voice sounding thick and scared and strangled all at the same time. "I'm in here."

He smiled in spite of himself. She was literal, too, like he was, which usually drove Luke nuts and sometimes even bothered Amanda. Amanda had one of those brains that jumped eight miles ahead at all times, and Kizzie was more of a brick-by-brick person.

Like Mike.

The brick-by-brick approach did not help him here.

"I know, sweetie," he said. "May I come in?"

"It's a girl's room," Kizzie said, and now the guard

smiled. It was fond, and somehow Mike found that fondness reassuring.

"I know, honey," he said, "but a boy can come in during tough times as long as he has permission."

"Can he?" Kizzie asked, and Mike could only assume she was asking Principal Hallenbeck.

"Yes, Kizzie, he can," Principal Hallenbeck said.

"Make sure no one else uses this bathroom," Mike said to the guard, and then pushed the door open.

The bathroom was spacious. It had six stalls, all on the right, and four sinks, all on the left, along with paper towel holders and one large overflowing garbage can.

Still, it felt off to him because everything was built at child scale. The sink counter came up to his hips. The mirror went so far down that it almost looked like there were other people in the room.

There weren't. Just him and Principal Hallenbeck and Kizzie—who, when she saw him, launched herself forward and wrapped herself around him so tightly that it hurt.

"Don't let him get me, Mike, please. Don't let him get me."

Mike looked over her head at Principal Hallenbeck. The woman was younger than he was, with dyed blond hair that curled beneath her ears. Her dark skin was lightly dusted with something sparkly, the kind of whimsy that made her a good leader for little kids, even though her outfit—some kind of pantsuit—made her look businesslike and efficient.

She wore a pair of glasses that magnified her hazel eyes, as well as the slight frown between them.

"Luke has to get off campus," Mike said in a soft voice, adult to adult.

"I know," Principal Hallenbeck said. "We called the police. They'll be here soon. Arresting him for trespass won't stick. We've had this kind of issue before and..."

She let her voice trail off, but Mike understood what she was saying. She was saying she could only do so much.

Hell, the system could only do so much.

"Please, Uncle Mike. I don't want him here," Kizzie said into his side, her voice muffled.

He understood why she didn't want her father here. She loved school. It was one of two safe places in her world. The other one was Mike's condo.

He put his arms around her and held her tight, but he didn't take his gaze off Principal Hallenbeck.

"I could take her home," he said, "but I think right now, she's safer here, especially if you have a guard with her."

"That's unusual," Principal Hallenbeck said, her frown growing deeper.

"I know," Mike said, "but the whole situation is odd. Luke knows better than to come here in the middle of a school day."

Mike let that last sentence hang, hoping that Principal Hallenbeck would understand what wasn't said. *Luke knows better...so why was he here?*

But Mike didn't say that out loud because he didn't

want to scare Kizzie more than she already was. Something was really off. It almost felt like part of a plan, but what could the plan be?

Mike wasn't usually overly sensitive or paranoid. He also wasn't the kind of person to react badly to a single conversation or a single word (*annihilate*), but he was scared. Deeply and profoundly scared.

Principal Hallenbeck took a deep breath, closed her eyes for a moment, and then opened them, as if she had come to a decision.

"One day," she said. "We can do this for one day. Otherwise, you know private schools…"

She didn't finish, because she turned the tables on him. Clearly this time, she assumed he would understand. And he did. The really rich in this city had their kids go to some private schools, not for the education, but for the security features.

He didn't want that for Kizzie, but if it was necessary to protect her, then so be it.

"One day. Today," he said. "I'll have a solution by the time I pick her up."

Kizzie was shaking her head as she clung to him. "No," she said. "I don't want you to go, Uncle Mike."

He thought about it for a moment, wondering if he could take her to his place. He'd have to stay with her, and right now, something was poking at his brain, making him restless.

That feeling was growing worse. He needed to act. He

absolutely needed to, and he couldn't do that while physically protecting Kizzie.

"I know you don't want me to go, sweetheart," he said. "But I need to solve this."

The word *I* brought him up short, even as he spoke it. His heart knew before his brain that he was the only one who could solve this. Jasper had helped with that.

Amanda wasn't interested in solving the problem of Luke and Kizzie, and Luke, well, Jasper had been right. To Luke, Kizzie was the prize.

Kizzie squeezed so hard that Mike was beginning to think he'd have black-and-blue child-sized fingerprints on his sides. She was shaking.

Maybe he should just take her out of the city.

The thought enticed him for a moment, before it stopped him short. He wouldn't put it past Gary to try and get Mike arrested for kidnapping. And then Mike wouldn't be able to help Kizzie at all.

Mike rubbed his hand on Kizzie's back, trying to calm her, just like he had done when she was a baby. He had no idea what would make this day better. He also had not realized just how terrified of her father Kizzie had become.

She finally stopped shaking. So Mike slid his fingers between her hands and his shirt, ungluing her from him. Then he held her hands in his as he crouched down until he was at her eye level.

She didn't look like the little girl he had seen the day

before. Her face was swollen from crying, her eyes red. Her lower lip trembled.

"I don't want Daddy to get me," she said for the third time.

"Kiz," Mike said, his voice calm. He needed information. Something had changed.

He knew how to ask questions that wouldn't plant anything in her head. He had talked to Jasper about that too, and Jasper had given him some tips.

Gently, Mike asked, "Did something different happen recently?"

She blinked, and a tear escaped. Her bow-shaped mouth was an upside-down U, so very sad that it broke Mike's heart.

"Daddy called last night," she said. "I didn't answer. Mommy doesn't want me to answer."

Neither did Mike, but as with this entire thing, he had no real say in it.

"So he left a message." Kizzie swallowed hard. Her bloodshot eyes remained on his. He couldn't remember ever seeing her this intense.

"What kind of message?" Mike asked.

"It's on my phone," she said, but she wasn't letting go of his hands so that she—or he—could grab the phone.

"I can get it," Principal Hollenbeck said, but Mike met her gaze and shook his head ever so slightly. He recognized the look in Kizzie's face. The very thought of that message scared her.

He turned his attention back to Kizzie.

"Tell me about that message," he said, working as hard as he could to keep his voice level.

"It started all normal," she said, "you know, that he missed me and stuff, and then he said—" her voice hitched, and her eyes filled with tears. "—he said…my mom…was keeping me from him and she didn't have the right to do that, and then he started yelling, and, I stopped listening, Mike. Mommy's lawyer says I can't delete stuff, but I want to delete that."

Mike nodded. Fury rose in him, and he no longer trusted his own voice. At least he had learned along the way how to keep his expression neutral, so Kizzie couldn't see the anger.

"He didn't call her my mom," Kizzie said. "He used the 'b' word, Uncle Mike. He called her—"

"I understand, Kiz," Mike said, careful to keep his voice low. He'd heard Luke call Amanda that for years. The fact that it had finally slipped out to his daughter disturbed Mike.

Luke knew better than that too.

"Can you let Principal Hallenbeck play that message for the police?" he asked.

"No," Kizzie said. "I'm not supposed to play my messages for anyone."

"Who told you that?" Mike asked.

"Daddy," Kizzie said. "I'm not even supposed to play them for Mommy."

Principal Hallenbeck raised her hand and adjusted her glasses before rubbing her chin. Both of those were clearly nervous gestures. Her gaze met Mike's, and her mouth thinned.

She seemed just as angry as Mike about all of this.

He made himself focus on Kizzie.

"Can we tell the police about the message?" Mike asked.

"No," Kizzie said. "Daddy says they already hate him. I'm not supposed to do anything that'll make it worse."

The fury almost bubbled out of Mike's throat and into his mouth. But somehow he still managed to keep his tone even.

"You can't do anything to hurt your dad with the police," Mike said. "If they have a problem with your dad, it's because of things he's done."

Or is doing, Mike wanted to add but didn't. He didn't want Kizzie to think about that, to be even more scared than she already was.

Principal Hallenbeck raised a finger over Kizzie's head.

Mike nodded ever so slightly, giving Principal Hallenbeck permission to join this part of the conversation.

"I would like to mention this to the police," Principal Hallenbeck said in a very reasonable voice, "so that they won't allow your daddy to come back to the school. Is that all right?"

The two ideas had a war on Kizzie's face. She clearly wanted her father to stay away from here and she wanted to honor his unreasonable request.

Mike was having a tough time controlling the adrenaline in his body. He wanted to take physical action against his old frat brother, which was not something Mike would ever have contemplated in the past.

Maybe if he could just shake some sense into Luke...

"Is it okay, Mike?" Kizzie asked.

It took Mike a moment to escape that half-assed violent daydream and come back to the conversation. Was it all right for the principal to give the message to the police to keep Luke away from the school?

"Yes," Mike said. "We want your daddy as far from here as possible. Sometimes that means making hard choices. Those choices aren't always the ones other people want us to make."

Her little chin squared up—her determined look. She nodded once, the movement so adult that it broke his heart.

"Okay," she said to Principal Hallenbeck. "You can tell them."

"Thank you," Principal Hallenbeck said. Then her gaze met Mike's. "You're sure you can handle this by end of business...?"

No, he wasn't sure. How could he be sure?

"Yes," he said.

"Okay," Principal Hallenbeck said to Kizzie. "Let's get you cleaned up and back to class."

That war reappeared on Kizzie's face. She didn't want to go to class. She didn't want to leave Mike. He could feel it in the tightness of her fingers, in the way her eyes held his.

"Mike," Kizzie said, her voice thick. "What do I tell my friends?"

How the hell should he know? Then he realized her question was in part a worry and in part a ploy to keep him in this humid bathroom just a moment longer.

He wished Jasper were beside him to give him advice. But Jasper hadn't talked to him about something like this, not ever. So he tried to channel Jasper as best he could.

"Tell your friends that your dad is having a bad day," Mike said. "And that it's being handled and you'll tell them the whole story later."

"When later?" his Kizzie, the literal girl, asked.

"When we decide," Mike said. "Not today."

She frowned again, and then the frown faded. "Okay," she said. Apparently what he had said was good enough. "That's what we'll do."

And with that, the next steps were decided.

It still took a good ten minutes to get Kizzie out of that bathroom. Principal Hallenbeck and Mike both helped Kizzie wash her face, and gather herself.

"You don't have to be perfect," Mike said. "You just have to be you."

He had no real idea what that meant, but it sounded

good. And Principal Hallenbeck had run with it, talking about the ways that schedules and work and normal things like being in a classroom helped on the most difficult days.

It sounded like she was speaking from experience.

Mike finally managed to slip out of the bathroom. The guard was still there, staring at the old-fashioned clock built into the wall at the top of the stairs.

"Fifteen minutes until the bell," the guard said. "You think she'll get out of there before that?"

He was probably worried about the other kids going into the bathroom.

"I do," Mike said. "If not, remind them about five minutes before."

"Where are you going?" the guard asked.

"I'm going to shut this problem off at the root," Mike said. Even he didn't know what that meant, but it sounded good.

The guard frowned. It seemed like he was about to say something, but Mike spoke first.

"Please, protect my girl," Mike said, and then winced at his own word choice. But the guard didn't seem to notice. And he had probably heard everything from the conversation inside, including the fact that Kizzie had called him Uncle Mike.

"I will," the guard said solemnly.

"Don't let her out of your sight," Mike said. "And if her father or her uncle Gary show up, don't let them near her. Call Principal Hallenbeck, and then call me."

The guard frowned just a little. "All right," he said. "Anyone else?"

A chill ran through Mike. He hadn't been close to Luke in a long time. Mike knew that Luke's college friends as well as his legal colleagues had abandoned him, but Mike didn't know if Luke had substituted some shadier friends for the ones he lost.

Mike no longer knew who to name at all.

"Use your best judgment," Mike said. "I'm trusting it."

The guard straightened, almost like he was coming to attention. "I come here every day thinking I might have to protect these kids with my life."

Mike swallowed. He hadn't thought of that. Of course, the good security guards at elementary schools would make that assumption these days. What kind of world had this country moved into?

What kind of world had *he* moved into?

"You can trust that I'll be guarding her the same way," the guard said and then clarified, "With my life," as if Mike might miss the point.

And considering how distracted he was, how scared he was, he might have.

"Thank you," he said, making sure the guard knew he meant it. "I'll be back before school's out."

And then Mike hurried down the hall, taking the central stairs this time because he was going to go to the principal's office first, to get Luke the hell off this property.

The principal's office was down a tiny alcove in the

middle of the school. On the schematics, the office looked like an island in the middle of the interior courtyard.

In practice, the office felt like the hub of a completely different business, one that had nothing to do with children or education. The shades on the interior windows were closed—the better to protect someone who got called to the office—and the door was made of thick blond wood. The door knob was at adult height, unlike some of the doors in the main school corridor, and there was a full-size water fountain between one door and another marked *Private*.

A sign on the main door read *Office of the Principal,* and another below it said *Please Knock,* so Mike did. A buzzer sounded, which he guessed meant he could enter the room. As he did that, he realized he had never come to the principal's office in Harry S. by himself. He had always come with someone else, and the door had always been slightly open.

He turned the knob and pushed the door inward, expecting to see Luke sitting across from the receptionist's big blond desk. But Luke wasn't here.

Mike wasn't certain how many other rooms there were in this part of the office, but he didn't see Luke anywhere. The back part of the room—the part where the actual office was—contained one person: a police officer who was sitting in the chair opposite the principal's desk. The officer looked unconcerned about anything. He was actually scrolling through his phone.

"Where's Luke?" Mike asked the secretary.

The secretary, whose name was Zander, tilted his head a little, which made his spiky purple hair move almost like a weapon. He had a nose ring and a tattoo that crept up his neck like a beautifully designed skin rash.

Parents used to complain about him until they realized he was a highly competent man who adored the kids under his charge.

"We don't know," Zander said.

"What?" Mike asked. He had just left Kizzie with the principal and the guard. They might not be enough. He would have to go back, and probably take her home.

"Please don't worry, Mr. Cummings," Zander said. "I don't think Mr. Brocato is on the property any longer."

Mike shook his head, as if that would help make the words make more sense.

"You have a reason for that?" His tone wasn't as calm as he liked, as evidenced by the reaction of the police officer.

The man put his phone down and looked in the direction of the reception desk.

"Mr. Brocato fled when he heard you were coming," Zander said.

"Fled," Mike repeated. He was so jittery that he had to move sideways just to keep himself from pounding his fists on the desk's top.

"Yes, sir." Zander's voice was soft, soothing, probably the voice he used with the angry parents of crying children. "He went out the front and security cameras showed him heading toward his car which is gone now."

Mike almost demanded to know why he hadn't been told this, but maybe Principal Hallenbeck didn't know either. Maybe his assumption about her and her secretary being in constant contact was wrong.

"Unfortunately," Zander said—and his word choice made Mike even more jittery— "Mr. Brocado knew where the dead zones are in the cameras. We never saw him getting in his vehicle. The police showed up a few moments after he left, and I told them he was dangerous, and they needed to make sure he's gone."

The police officer came out of the back, tucking his phone into a pocket on his shirt. He was older, with lines that ran along his eyes all the way to his downturned mouth.

"I'm Officer Reese," he said. "And you are?"

"Oh, this is Mr. Cummings," Zander said in a slightly different tone. This one had to be for the authorities. "He's one of two people on Kizzie's contact list, the other being her mother."

"May I see some identification?" Reese said.

Mike wanted to shout that all of this was unnecessary, he had to figure out what was going on, he had to find Luke and he had to protect Kizzie, but instead of saying any of that, he reached into his back pants pocket, pulled out his wallet, and flipped it open to his driver's license.

Reese peered at it.

"Mr. Cummings has been one of Kizzie's main supports for years," Zander said. "He often picks her up from school. When we learned that Mr. Brocado was here, we contacted Mrs. Brocado, but we couldn't reach her, so as per long-standing instructions, we contacted Mr. Cummings."

"You're her stepfather?" Reese asked.

"No," Mike said. "I am considered part of the family. I was even in the birthing room the day Kizzie was born."

And her father wasn't. Mike didn't dare say anything else. He couldn't sound defensive, or he might get arrested or detained.

Reese frowned, then pushed the wallet back at Mike.

"He's authorized to speak for the family when Mrs. Brocado is not here," Zander said. "If you would like to see the paperwork…"

"That would probably be wise, considering all that is happening here," Reese said.

Mike made himself breathe. He needed things to be by the book, but he also needed to get out of there. Or get back to Kizzie. Or do *something*.

Zander pulled out a paper file with Kizzie's name on the flap and passed it to Reese. He bent over it for a moment and paused on a judge's order forbidding Luke Brocado from having any contact with his child on school grounds.

Then Reese sighed and pushed the paperwork away. He had probably seen too many incidents like this in his career.

Mike made himself breathe. He wanted to ask questions. He wanted to leave. But he had to exercise a patience he didn't really have so that he didn't make this incident worse.

"All right," Reese said. "Here's what I know."

He paused, theatrically? Dramatically? Or maybe just to take a breath himself so that he could choose the correct words.

"Luke Brocado was on this property unlawfully. He came to the principal's office on his own but left when he realized that you were coming."

Mike wanted to say, *Yes, I know. Zander just told me.*

"He went out front and rounded the building to get to his vehicle, but we were unable to track his movements clearly on the security cameras. His vehicle is now gone, but we couldn't tell from the cameras if he was behind the wheel. There is some evidence that he was not alone."

Mike couldn't restrain himself now. "What kind of evidence?"

He didn't sound as panicked as he felt, but he was sure he was probably wild-eyed.

"The place where Mr. Brocado parked is in the shade, and there might have been movement inside the vehicle while he was in the building." Reese's voice was totally dispassionate, as if none of this was a problem.

It was a hell of a problem. Mike did not know what Luke was about, but it couldn't be good.

"We are looking for the vehicle now, as well as

combing the grounds for Mr. Brocado," Reese said. "We also have officers in the building. Your daughter will be safe."

Mike's brain snapped into lawyer mode. Part of him admired the way that Reese sought information. Apparently, he thought that Mike was Kizzie's biological father, probably from an affair.

"She's not my daughter," Mike said. "But she is family."

"My mistake," Reese said in that same dispassionate voice. "My point is that we will find Mr. Brocado, and we will protect young Kizzie. We won't leave these premises until we're certain he's not here."

"Thank you," Mike said. He wasn't sure exactly how to proceed here. "Luke is pretty unstable. I'm also worried about Amanda—Mrs. Brocado. He's already got an assault charge because he hit her so hard—"

"I saw that," Reese said. "We're considering him dangerous. Do you know where Mrs. Brocado is?"

"I don't," Mike said, "and it's not like her to fail to answer her phone."

"We tried to call her first," Zander said. "She hasn't answered all morning."

Something flickered on Reese's face, and in that look, Mike saw something that made him think of Jasper's face as he said the word *annihilate*.

Mike's mouth went dry.

"You need to check on her," Mike said. "This isn't like her."

"I will make sure that someone goes to her home imme-diately," Reese said. "We will do our best to find her."

"Thank you," Mike said.

Reese held his radio, but before he clicked it, he said, "I would like to keep you here, Mr. Cummings. It's probably not safe for you to be out there either. It is sounding like Mr. Brocado is not stable."

Not stable. Of course he wasn't stable. He hadn't been stable for a long time.

But Mike didn't say that either, because he might erupt in fury.

"I'll stay away from my place until you find Luke," he said. "But I have one errand to run—"

"We don't want you in the middle of this, Mr. Cummings," Reese said. "Let us handle Mr. Brocado."

"Oh, I will," Mike said. "Believe me, I will."

He was not the athletic type. Even in college, he hadn't been able to best Luke at anything athletic. Mike certainly didn't want to try now.

He was about to explain that his errand was related, but not something that would get in the way, but then, he real-ized, he was going to sound defensive.

He reached into the back of his wallet, which he still held in one hand, and took out his business card.

"Please call me with any developments," he said, like the attorney he was. That part, at least, felt normal. And then he turned to Zander. "And please, Zander, let me know if you need anything for Kizzie or if I need to come back. My phone will be on all the time. I'm going to be reachable no matter what."

There it was, that tinge of panic. But Mike was entitled, right? This was one of the scariest situations he had been in in his entire life.

"Remember what I said, Mr. Cummings," Reese said.

Mike nodded. He almost said, *Remember that you promised to keep Kizzie safe*, but he didn't. That actually sounded passive-aggressive, and he needed the police on his side.

He thanked them both again, and walked out of the principal's office more upset than when he had gone in.

"What the hell are you doing, Luke?" Mike muttered to himself. "What the hell is going on?"

Mike made himself walk to his Porsche just so that he could calm down. The eleven o'clock bell had rung, but a few kids were still standing near their lockers. One little boy ran by, the sudden movement startling Mike.

A police officer stood near the entrance Mike had originally used—looking, not bored exactly, but not engaged either. At least, until Mike started down the hall.

"Sir, may I see some identification?" the officer asked.

Mike almost said, *I'm leaving*, but then he realized that this request made perfect sense if Luke was loose in the building.

Mike opened his wallet again, saying, "I'm on my way out. I will be back."

The officer nodded as if he didn't care, then looked at the identification the way a bartender would look at a possibly fake I.D.—one glance at Mike, another at the license, then a second look at Mike.

The officer handed the wallet back and said nothing else.

Mike left, feeling just a little unnerved.

As he stepped outside into the gray morning, he wondered why that unnerved him. The police presence should have made him feel better.

Maybe unnerved was his default now.

He had certainly been unnerved when he parked. The Porsche sprawled over three parking spaces. And when he arrived, he had thought that he had parked well, if hastily.

His perceptions were not just heightened, but off, and that bothered him. He wanted to be making good decisions, not decisions that he would question later.

He got into the car, and put his phone in the center console before leaning his head back. He had to calm down. He wasn't good to anyone if he panicked.

He made himself breathe, and then he made a mental list.

He needed to figure out a place for himself, Amanda, and Kizzie to stay—maybe for the night, maybe longer. It couldn't be somewhere that Luke knew about.

And he needed to stop Luke. This kind of police presence wasn't going to last past the morning, especially if Luke hadn't done more than trespass on school grounds.

Mike needed to get ahold of Amanda's attorney. She could ask for more resources to be spent on this, and maybe even get the police to rearrest Luke, since this could be considered a violation of his bail.

Mike let out a breath, then reminded himself he only had a few hours to figure out what to do next. He'd start with the lawyer and then work his way through. Maybe he'd get hotel rooms for Amanda and Kizzie and himself. They'd have to be expensive rooms with good security.

Maybe this entire scary thing might convince Amanda to take up Georgina's offer and move to North Dakota.

He made himself breathe in and then out one more time. He didn't feel relaxed, but he wasn't as panicked. He sat all the way up and saw movement by the trees. Luke?

Then Mike squinted and realized he was seeing officers, combing the woods just like they had promised.

Just like the police officer near the door, seeing the others should have calmed him, but it didn't. It made him realize that everyone—including the police—understood the stakes.

Mike grabbed his phone and scrolled through his contacts. When he'd used the AI to call Amanda's attorney, it had called the law firm. This time, he searched until he found Serena Tomlinson's name and next to it the words *personal cell*. He called that first, but it rang and rang before going to voicemail, which meant the phone was either off or she wasn't tending to it.

He left a sharp and pointed message, telling Tomlinson that this was an emergency and he needed to hear from her immediately. Then he called the reception desk and asked pointedly if the legal secretary had given Tomlinson the message that Mike had left earlier.

"I did," the secretary said. "She told me she'd call when the deposition was on a break which should be...soon."

The pause was clearly her checking her watch or the time or something.

"Tell her to call me," Mike said.

And hung up, feeling angry and helpless and panicked all over again.

Then he looked at his own watch. It would only take him ten minutes or so to get to Tomlinson's office on the wealthier side of town.

If he took the back roads, it might take even less time.

He started up the Porsche, its roaring purr suggesting that the car was as anxious to get moving as he was.

He peeled out of the parking lot like the teenager he no longer was, and drove as fast as he safely could through the back streets. Fortunately, he was going through a development that had failed halfway through construction, so the roads were good but there was no possibility for children on the road.

He squealed around an access road, went behind the

empty softball fields, and pulled up at the back of the three-story building that looked more like a house than an office complex. The parking lot disabused that notion though. There were parking spots reserved for various lawyers, other spots reserved for the physical therapists on the first floor, and even more reserved for the dentists on the second. The parking spaces for clients were equally segmented.

He was careful not to park in the handicapped zones, but he took one of the attorney's close parking spaces, figuring that asking forgiveness was easier than asking for permission. And maybe, even, at this time of day, no one would notice.

He made sure he didn't straddle three parking spots this time, though, and shut off the car, wishing he could leap out of it like Tom Cruise in a *Mission: Impossible* movie. Instead, Mike got out like a normal human being and scanned the parking lot for any sign of Luke's POS.

There were half a dozen cars that he didn't recognize, some of them spendier than his, probably belonging to the other lawyers in the deposition, and some of them late model SUVs and sedans, probably belonging to the patients of the dentists and physical therapists.

Then he saw Gary's car, which wasn't quite the P.O.S. that his brother's was, but it wasn't the kind of car a successful attorney drove. It was an ancient Volvo that didn't even have collector's value. He always claimed that the most recent ex had gotten the "good" car in the divorce, but that divorce had been years ago. Gary had

had more than enough time to replace his ride—and he hadn't. The Brocado brothers were apparently hurting for money.

The panic had lodged in Mike's throat. If Gary was here, then Amanda probably was too. Mike walked to the far edge of the parking lot, where clients who didn't want to be seen usually parked so they could use the side entrance, and sure enough, Amanda's white minivan was parked as close to the door as possible.

Mike wasn't sure if he felt relieved or upset, and then he realized, if Gary was here and Amanda was here, then Luke knew where his soon-to-be ex was. The police at her house were as useless as Mike on a baseball field.

He called Zander, and asked if Reese was still in the office.

"Yes," Zander said.

"Let me speak to him," Mike said, and the phone rustled as Zander handed it over, Zander's very soft *Mike Cummings needs to speak to you* sounding very far away.

"Yeah," Reese said into the phone, as if he didn't want to be bothered.

"Amanda Brocado is not at her house," Mike said. "She's at her attorney's office along with Luke's brother. Please send some of that protection here."

"You're there?" Reese asked.

"I need to talk with her attorney who has been in a deposition all day. I wanted to get her to press charges against Mike. But I haven't been able to reach her—"

A loud bang resounded from inside the building, followed rapidly by another and another.

Gunshots.

"What the hell is that?" Reese asked.

"I don't know," Mike said. "I'm going to see."

And he hung up.

He was already running into the building, phone in hand, thinking he shouldn't have hung up, but it was too late to redial. He pulled open the door only to have people run and hobble past him, most of them screaming. One of them was a young doctor with the name of the physical therapy office on his smock. He was clutching a cell phone.

"Call 911," Mike yelled as people passed him. He clearly wasn't the only one who thought the noises were gunshots. "Call 911!"

He took the stairs up the second floor two at a time, having to lean against the banister a few times as dental patients, wearing those little paper smocks, scurried down. One was a woozy-looking woman who still had bloody wads of dental pads sticking out of her mouth. For a moment, Mike thought she had been shot, but there was a dental assistant beside her, holding her up, saying, "You'll be fine, you'll be just fine. Let's get you outside."

People poured out of that office, silently, looking terrified. Inside the half-open door, he could see a woman—clearly an assistant or a secretary—on a landline, shouting that they needed the police.

One guy pushed past Mike, taking the stairs two at a

time, looking determined. He was the only person who didn't seem terrified, but he was moving like someone who was terrified—hurrying away as if his life depended on it.

Mike continued up one more flight of stairs, his heart pounding. Tomlinson was part of a large and prestigious law firm that covered the entire top floor. The stairs opened into a seating area beneath a skylight, where—on good days—Mike had seen attorneys and clients sitting in overstuffed barrel-shaped chairs, reading in natural light.

There were some papers on the floor near the chairs, but no people. Maybe he had already seen them scurrying down the stairs as he came up.

The third floor was eerily quiet. No screaming, no more bangs…and no one fleeing.

His mouth was dry.

He stood behind the ornate wooden door, and slowly pulled it open, half expecting a gunshot, like in the movies. But so far, nothing except some Bach floating across a sound system and something that might have been whimpering.

He eased himself inside. The desks were empty. Chairs were overturned.

The shots had come from here.

A high heel shoe was on its side near the reception desk. More papers littered the floor, and a Starbucks cup had fallen over, its grayish brownish contents dripping onto the carpet below, making the air smell of coffee and caramel.

His heart was pounding and he knew he probably shouldn't go any farther, but he did, because Amanda's car was here and this was her attorney's office and Gary was here and something bad had happened, and Mike couldn't stand outside imagining it. He had to face it, and face it now.

The conference room was on the corner of the building, where some of the larger offices were. He'd been in that room a few times during the early stages of Luke and Amanda's divorce, back when Gary was convinced that Mike had been the cause of the marital troubles.

The silence seemed even more profound here. The classical music continued—maybe that wasn't Bach. Maybe it was Handel. It didn't matter; he would never be able to hear that piece of music again without its precise, measured notes being a counterpoint to the empty mess he was seeing everywhere.

He had a sense that he was not alone, that everyone in this office was hiding instead of fleeing. But he didn't search for them, and he didn't say anything.

Instead, he rounded a corner—and there was the conference room. One of the exterior glass windows had shattered, clearly from a bullet, and inside there, he could hear more whimpering. Blood dripped along one wall, and a person—a woman—was draped over the conference table as if she had fallen asleep in the middle of the deposition.

The door was open, oddly enough, and blood footprints led away from the room.

He was careful not to step on them. He moved to one side, and crept forward, before remembering that he still held his cell phone.

This time, it was his turn to call 911, and the dispatch answered quickly.

"We need ambulances at the offices of Terry, Tomlinson, and Egrean," he said.

"We've already dispatched an ambulance to that location," the woman dispatcher said.

"We're going to need more," he said. "I'm in the office now, and it's a blood bath."

"You need to leave, sir," the woman said. "We will be there in less than two minutes. Let the officials handle…"

He didn't hear the rest because he stuck the phone in the back pocket of his pants, without hanging up this time. He stuck his hands in his front pockets so that he wouldn't touch anything and accidentally contaminate the scene.

"Amanda?" he asked, sounding as scared as he felt.

He heard whimpering, but he didn't see her.

A man was sprawled on the rug near a toppled chair. His face was turned sideways, but he appeared to be lying in a gigantic bloodstain. No one would voluntarily do that.

He thought he heard voices.

"Amanda?" he repeated. He couldn't tell who the woman was who had face-planted on the table, but she was too thin to be Amanda. Her hair was too dark.

The voices got closer, and then someone grabbed him, making him jump.

"Come with us, sir," said a woman, and she manhandled him away from the open door.

"I know people in there," he said, and hearing himself, he sounded stupid, but he felt stupid. His brain had slowed to a crawl. He couldn't let it slow like that. He needed to think.

"I'm sure you do know people, sir," the woman said. Her voice was soothing, but businesslike at the same time. He looked at her. She was in a police uniform. "Are you hurt?"

More police officers hurried past her, pausing at the door, guns drawn. She pulled Mike away, leading him back the way he came.

"Are you hurt?" she asked again.

"No, no," he said, wanting to shake her off. But he knew better. They were the authorities. They knew how to solve this. "I'm not hurt. I just got here and called you all, asking for more ambulances. I—"

He wanted to say he had come from the school, but that wasn't relevant, at least to this. He would talk to a detective or someone else. Because…Luke…

Instead, Mike said, "You're going to need to get medical personnel up here. I know people in that room. And some-one's crying, someone's—"

"We've got this, sir," the police officer said, slow-walking him to the main door. "Please exit the building so we can handle it. There will be someone outside who can take your statement."

Statement. He nodded. He had to make a statement. It seemed so minor, considering what was going on.

But he was only going to be in the way. He knew that. Intellectually, he knew that. But he wanted to run back to the conference room, he wanted to find Amanda, he wanted to assure himself that she wasn't there.

It took all of his self-control to slip out the door. He walked down the stairs because he didn't want to barrel into the first responders. They were still coming in, some of them, scattering as they came in the door, some going to the offices on the first floor, others coming up the stairs, some going even farther down hallways that Mike hadn't realized existed until right now.

He made it to the second floor, saw that the dentist office's door was still open, but no one was inside, except one police officer, standing at the entrance, facing inward. Other officers were working the hallway, gathering near the elevator, and one was holding the door open to the nearby bathroom.

He didn't linger, but he didn't hurry. His heart was aching, and he was still breathing hard from his trip up those stairs. Or maybe from panic that he wasn't sure he should acknowledge. Tinny radio voices sounded in the cavernous area below, and the main doors were open, letting in some warmer air from outside.

More first responders came up the stairs, but no EMTs. Apparently the building had to be cleared first. He wanted to yell, *Hurry! They're dying up there!* but Sensible Mike understood the need for caution. Real Mike wanted to pivot and run back up, screaming at them to follow him.

He made it to the first floor when another officer, small and male, grabbed his arm and asked him if he was all right.

The lie was, *Yes, yes, I'm just fine,* but they weren't asking about his mental state. They were asking about his physical one. So, he spoke the lie, "Yes, yes, I'm fine," and they hurried him outside, where a dozen EMTs stood, hands on one side of a medical gurney, large square bags clearly filled with equipment underneath it.

"Sir," said an officer, another woman, with a hard face and sun-induced wrinkles, "we need you to make a statement."

He nodded as she led him away from the building, near what he used to think of as an unnecessary grouping of trees that had been planted in the middle of the parking lot.

There, another woman stood with a recorder and a notepad. The woman who brought him there was the one interviewing him. She asked his name, his reason for being there, and that was when he decided to come clean.

"I came to talk to Serena Tomlinson," he said. "I couldn't reach her on the phone. She's the divorce lawyer for my friend Amanda. I am on her—Amanda's—school list as one of the trusted people to contact and Harry S. contacted me because Kizzie's father—Amanda's daughter Kizzie—he showed up at the school unannounced. He's out on bail for an assault charge and he's not supposed to go near the school, so I went to make sure nothing happened, and I've been trying to call both Amanda and Serena all morning—and I didn't know they were both in that room, that they're both..."

His voice cracked. It couldn't crack. He had to get through this. Kizzie was going to need him. And he was going to have to focus.

He looked at the building. Some first responders were circling it, as if they were searching, but the EMTs were starting to mobilize. More police vehicles reached the parking lot, blocking off the entrance and exit. Someone was stringing crime scene tape everywhere, and the press had shown up. They were down the road, being held back by some kind of police barricade.

"Luke," he said, gathering himself and looking at the officer with the harsh face, "he left the school before I did. I don't know why he wasn't here, if they were having a deposition on his divorce case. His brother Gary is here—at least his car is here—and I think..." (*I think I saw him on the floor, face down in his own blood, but I'm not sure, I'm not sure.*) "...maybe he was in that room. I don't know."

"All right, Mr. Cummings." The officer's voice wasn't quite soothing, but it was calm, certainly calmer than he was. "I'm going to call the school—"

"You have officers there," he said. "At least, there were. And they were looking for Luke."

"All right," she said. "Can you tell me what he drives?"

"It's a P.O.S.," he said, and then he realized that wasn't descriptive, so he did his best to describe the sedan. But he couldn't remember the license plate. It wasn't a vanity plate, it was just numbers and letters, and his voice was going up and—

The officer put a gentle hand on his arm. "It's not here, Mr. Cummings," she said. "It's not here. I will get in touch with our officers at the school and see what they know."

She beckoned another officer over and then moved slightly away from Mike, so that she could relay information about Luke.

Mike made himself breathe. His heart had settled down, but he felt like he had run a marathon. He had to get a grip on his brain. Kizzie was going to need him.

Kizzie. Her mother had been in that room. And he had no idea if Amanda was alive. Kizzie was going to need him. She had no other family in this town. Just him…and Luke.

Mike let out another breath. He had told the police about Luke twice now. They'd find him. He couldn't get Kizzie, could he?

Mike was about to reach for his phone when the other officer, the one who was recording and taking notes, said, "Just give her a minute, and we'll finish with you. Then you can call someone."

He looked at the officer, frowned, wondering who he needed to give a minute, then realized it was the hard-faced officer. Oh, he was not doing well.

The hard-faced officer returned. "They're looking for

Luke Brocado," she said. "They haven't found him yet, but they now realize that there might be more to his appearance there than initially thought."

"Kizzie," Mike said. "What about Kizzie?"

"The school is on a soft lockdown. No one can go in without permission, and they have that under tight control. No one has left either, so I would venture a guess that your girl is all right."

A guess. That was all he was going to get was some officer's guess? He had to get there.

"I'd like to finish up and go to the school," he said.

"I understand that, Mr. Cummings. We're going to need more from you, though. I need to know what, if anything, that you saw."

"Just what your officers are seeing," he said. "I was in this parking lot when I heard the shots. In fact, I was on the line with the officer at the school because Gary's car was here, and Amanda's, and then the shots…"

He didn't remember hanging up. He grabbed his phone out of his back pocket, but the officer put up a hand.

"Go slow, Mr. Cummings. I need to know what you saw."

He glanced at his phone anyway. All he could see was the home screen. He had been disconnected. Of course he had. He had done it himself. He had called 911.

His brain was floating over so many details.

"What I saw?" he said. "I told you."

"I want to know if you saw anything suspicious."

"You mean, besides hearing gunshots and seeing everyone in the building running except the people I care about?"

"Yes," she said. That calm voice again. Not soothing, but not overwrought like he was.

And then his brain caught it. The one person who hadn't seemed panicked. He had seemed determined.

"There was one guy," Mike said, no longer looking at the cop. He looked at the edge of the little berm of trees, saw rocks and tiny pieces of broken glass in the parking spot directly in front of him. He focused on that, trying to see what he had noticed as he was running up the stairs while everyone else was running down.

The cop waited patiently. The second cop had her pen poised over her notepad.

"He was coming down from three, he was the only one I think I saw from three, because I know most everyone there, and they weren't running, I think they were hiding."

Mike couldn't be sure of that, though. He wanted to be sure, but there was nothing to be sure about. Not today.

"He took the steps down two at a time," Mike said, "and he didn't look panicked. He looked determined."

"Can you describe him?" the officer asked.

"White, skinny," Mike said. "Wasn't dressed up, like you know, you do when you come to a lawyer's office. He was hurrying past people, but—I only saw him for a moment, you know?"

"Yes, I do," the officer said. "Did you notice anything else?"

Mike thought. The glass in the parking lot wasn't helping him focus any longer.

"Just how different his reaction was from everyone else's. They were all scared and surprised." Mike raised his head. "This guy, he didn't look surprised."

"Had you ever seen him before?" the officer said.

Mike shook his head. "Not that I remember."

"What was he wearing?" the officer asked.

"Flannel shirt," Mike said, "which is weird because it's not that cold. Black t-shirt underneath, jeans."

"Good," she said. "Anything else?"

"I don't know. I can't—

"Was he holding anything?" she asked.

"No," Mike said. "Not that I saw. He didn't hold the banister either, coming down. Most people would, you know, when they're in a hurry? He didn't. He pushed past people, but other people were pushing too. He didn't seem to notice me."

Mike had just remembered that. The man didn't look at anyone else, just focused on getting out of the building— not that Mike blamed him. Everyone was focused on getting out.

"Are you all right with coming to the station? You'll have to give your statement again, and maybe talk to a sketch artist," the cop said. "If we don't have footage of the hallway, that is. We'll look for him."

"I can't go to the station right now," Mike said. "I promised Kizzie I'd go to the school. I promised Principal Hallenbeck. I can't break that promise, not now."

The hard-faced officer looked at the other one, as if they were silently communicating about something.

"Please," Mike said. "I know you usually keep people close, but I was on the phone with an officer. I called 911. You can track all of my movements. I *have* to get to Kizzie. Her mom's in there. God, what am I going to tell her about her mom?"

"Did you see her mother?" the hard-faced officer asked.

He thought, that scene, the whimpering. The woman sprawled over the table. The man (Gary?) with his face in his own blood.

"No," he said.

"Then right now, you don't say anything. We will send someone to the school to deal with the family as soon as we can."

It seemed to Mike like the hard-faced officer was making promises she couldn't keep.

"In the meantime, I will contact the school and let them know you're returning and that they should let you inside. Go directly there, Mr. Cummings. Don't stop anywhere else."

"Okay," he said.

She nodded once, gave him her card which he didn't know what to do with, so he stuck it in his wallet, and then she patted his arm.

"We will take care of your loved ones," she said.

He had no idea what that meant. The hard-faced officer started to move off, when he said, "My car is in the lot. How do I get out of here?"

"Ah," she said. "Take me to your car."

He looked over at it. The reserved spot he had chosen was in the middle of the staging area. Around it were ambulances and cop cars and now some kind of boxy vehicle with the words *Tactical Unit* emblazoned on the side.

Still, he could snake his way out if they let him.

"You're lucky," the cop said as Mike pointed out his spot. "Your vehicle has already been investigated and deemed clean."

He frowned before the words sank in. The police had checked the vehicle for bombs and probably other weapons as well.

"You will have to open the trunk," she said.

The trunk, such as it was, barely fit a suitcase. Porches like his were not made for hauling. They had been made to impress. No one was impressed this morning, but Mike had the sense that they would be happy if he got the Porsche out of their way.

He opened the trunk, and the cop inspected it while two others watched. Then she waved him on, pointed out that he could snake past the *Reserved* sign, drive behind the tactical vehicle, and then drive over a short curb that separated this parking lot from a lot that led into a high-end strip mall.

His Porsche rode low, and normally, he would have complained that he might damage the undercarriage driving out that way, but at the moment, he didn't care unless the damage prevented him from getting back to Harry S.

He slid into the Porsche, put his phone in its holder, and grabbed the gearshift when the cop knocked on his window. His heart sank. They weren't going to let him leave after all.

"Go directly to the school complex," she said. "They need you there."

He hadn't seen her talk to anyone or even speak on a radio or on her phone. He had no idea if there was news, and if there was, he wasn't going to get it, because she had already walked away.

He hesitated for a moment, thinking of chasing after her, and then rejected it. Patience. He was going to need patience today.

He put the Porsche in gear and eased out of the parking lot. Even more EMTs had arrived. People in uniform were scouring the back and sides of the building. There were more vehicles with red lights flashing than he had ever seen in a single area before.

He bumped over the curb and then found himself in that mostly empty parking lot. Unmarked police vehicles were pulling up, some of them with drivers who looked at him strangely, and they were parking here. So this area was going to be so full of people in authority that they would outnumber the people who had been inside the building.

He finally saw some of those people by chance. They were huddled near a ratty McDonald's in this parking lot, sitting on the outdoor tables. A few of them held McDonald's paper cups, and others were crying. There were officers with them, apparently trying to take statements just like his officer had done with him.

He drove to the opposite of the lot as far from the scene as he could get, encountering a police line, some police motorcycles parked sideways to block the road, and then a phalanx of media types, pressing against the police barricade as if they would take unified action to break through at any moment.

All of the reporters stared at him as he was allowed through the barricade, and some surrounded his car, making it hard to drive. He just kept pressing forward, ignoring the shouts of "Who are you?" "What's going on in there?" "Were you inside?"

His stomach clenched, and he gritted his jaw, careful to keep an even speed so that he didn't hit anyone. He knew that these reporters would grab his license and figure out who he was.

In a moment of clarity, he realized that he couldn't take Kizzie to his house even if someone had arrested Luke. The reporters would be there, and they would want a piece of Kizzie as well as a piece of Mike.

He swallowed compulsively, then continued forward, finally breaking out of the scrum and into an open street. Even the streets three blocks away were blocked off. More red lights, more police cars, the now-ubiquitous police motorcycles parked sideways so that no one could speed through.

He had no idea that this city had such a large police force. He hoped that not everyone was here, that someone was out searching for Luke.

Even though Mike hadn't seen Luke here, Mike was deep-down convinced that the disaster here was Luke's fault.

Mike drove back roads to the school complex, hearing more and more sirens coming from the main roads.

When he reached the base of the hill where the Complex was, he saw even more cars, and another police barricade. No reporters here, though. They hadn't figured out that the Complex was in lockdown or maybe (fortunately) the city didn't have as many reporters as it had police.

Parents were starting to show up, though. They came in SUVs and sedans, in heels and suits, in jeans and ball-caps, all looking terrified and stressed. A woman Mike vaguely recognized was pacing along the roadside berm, a phone in one hand as she gestured wildly with the other.

Mike pulled up as far as he could go and rolled down his window.

"Mike Cummings," he said with the most official tone he could manage. "I'm cleared to go inside."

The officer checked, which was good, because that meant if Luke had circled around somehow and was going to use this chaos to get back in, then he wouldn't make it through.

"You're cleared," the officer said and knocked loudly on the roof of the Porsche, making Mike jump.

He inched forward, making eye contact with each officer in charge of this part of the scene, until he reached the one who was in charge of pulling the barricade aside and letting the occasional car through.

Someone yelled behind him, which then turned into a chorus of "How come he can go through?" "I need to see my son!" "My daughter's in there. Let me through."

Mike rolled up the window, blocking out that noise, and eased up the hill, just in case he might come around a corner and accidentally hit someone.

The same cars were in the lot here, and there were only two extra police vehicles. He didn't see Luke's POS either, which was a relief. Mike hadn't realized he had expected to see the POS when he arrived.

He parked near the same spot as before, this time judiciously staying within one parking spot.

He got out of the Porsche and then checked himself to see if he had accumulated weird dirt or blood (blood!) from the Tomlinson office. His stomach flopped, and he willed it to behave.

He would think about all he had seen later, when he had the time and the crisis was over. Not now.

He walked carefully to the front doors, and the same officer who had been there before was there now, only standing outside. He held the door open for Mike, who wanted to say something, but didn't have the words.

Instead, he just nodded at the man, who nodded back. Then Mike went inside.

The smell of gym socks and peanut butter had faded, maybe because the airlock doors had been opening and closing so many times. He went inside, struck by the hush in the hallways.

The kids were still in classrooms, but they looked stressed now. They probably knew about the lockdown.

He'd been briefed on lockdowns at one point, and at Harry S, lockdowns were conducted to keep everyone in one place—the students inside the building and the world outside of it.

Harry S's policy, though, wasn't to gather the kids in the gym or the cafeteria, but to let them continue through their day, studying and learning—depending on the threat, of course.

He wasn't sure what they could learn in this environment, but he mentally applauded the effort, if only to keep the kids from ruminating on whatever was going on.

He made it to the center hallway, where the principal's office was. This time, the door was open. Reese was standing outside the door, talking to Principal Hallenbeck.

They heard Mike before they saw him, because they were looking down the hallway, Reese with his right hand on the top of his secured firearm.

When they saw that it was Mike, they both relaxed.

"Where's Kizzie?" he asked.

"In my office," Principal Hallenbeck said, and the words seemed heavy, wrong. Mike had thought Kizzie would be in a classroom like everyone else. "Someone told her about the law office."

For a second, Mike was angry that Kizzie had to deal with the news alone, and then Mike's mouth went dry. "Amanda?" he asked, thinking, *oh, shit, she was dead. She had died in that conference room and he had let her. He had heard her whimper and he hadn't helped her and now she was dead...*

"She's alive," Principal Hallenbeck said, clearly reading his expression, "but badly injured. They've taken her to Cedar Ridge Hospital because it has the best trauma unit."

And the only one in the city that had a lot of experience with gunshot wounds.

"She's in critical condition," Reese said. "They're not sure she'll make it."

"Should I go there?" Mike asked. "Take Kizzie there?"

He didn't think it was a good idea, because Luke might know where Amanda was, especially if Amanda hadn't changed her emergency contacts, and Kizzie would be even more traumatized, and what was Mike going to do if Amanda died?

"No," Reese said. "Don't take Kizzie to the hospital. We need to find Luke Brocado first."

That thought echoed Mike's, but then he honed in on the real point.

"You still haven't found Luke?" Mike asked.

"No," Reese said, "but we did find his car. It apparently died on him. He's on foot. We're searching."

At least they were still searching for Luke, even with—or maybe because of—everything that was going on.

"Where on foot are you looking?" Mike asked.

"The Arch Hill neighborhood," Reese said.

Mike let out a small breath. Arch Hill was right next to the university. More specifically, the neighborhood bordered Fraternity Row. The houses in Arch Hill were filled with old houses that had been repurposed into apartments that were usually crammed with too many students.

The hill itself was a party location, and it had some natural party spots. One was the basement of an old tower pressed up against a shallow cave. The frat that Mike and Luke both belonged to had taken over that shallow cave on hazing nights.

Mike had no idea if anyone still used the shallow cave, but even if they did, he doubted any college students would be inside it during the day.

"If that's the case," Mike said, "I think I know where he might be."

"His phone is pinging at the tower," Reese said, "but we can't find him."

The tower was a hundred-and-fifty year old structure that had been one of the first places built when the city was founded. For reasons no one in the city understood except a handful of frat boys, the tower had been built on the lower part of Arch Hill, not on the very top.

"You check the basement of the tower?" Mike asked, figuring that at least the police would know about the hidden sections of the tower.

"There's a basement?" Reese said.

Mike nodded. "It butts up against a shallow cave. The Beta Phi Fraternity has been using it for years."

Reese gave Mike a thin smile. "The Secret Society, eh?" he asked with a touch of bitterness. "You're a member?"

Mike hadn't heard Beta Phi called the Secret Society for years. But it was a secret society, modeled after some of the Ivy League frats. The upper levels of Beta Phi had layers that Mike never achieved. One of them was membership by tap only—which meant that one of the Beta Phi regular frat brothers might get tapped by someone in the upper echelon.

Mike had never been tapped, not that it bothered him. By the time he had become a junior, he hadn't wanted to be tapped. He had regretted being in Beta Phi, not because he was ethical, but because he wasn't social. He didn't like the constant partying and the noise.

He had actually moved out of the frat house that year, so that he could have quiet study time.

"I suppose I could still be considered a member," Mike

said. "I don't do any of the alumni things. Luke was a member in my years, though, and he was heavily involved."

"So he knows about this basement you claim is in the tower?" Reese asked.

"He was one of the people who took me there. I helped bring pledges up to the tower at the beginning of my junior year." Which was, Mike realized, when he really became disillusioned with the frat.

"Hmm," Reese said, and Mike could see some thoughts flitting across Reese's face. Mike could guess at what some of those thoughts were. He remembered, from his years in Beta Phi, that the frat was particularly proud of the way it had never been cited for hazing its members.

That was because most of the hazing had taken place at the tower.

"We have had several officers searching the base of the tower," Reese said. "The phone says Mr. Brocado's here, but we can't find him or the phone."

"Yeah," Mike said. "The door's not in the most obvious place."

"Can you tell me where it is?" Reese asked.

"I can," Mike said, "but even then, it's impossible to find. In my day, it was deliberately blocked, so that only people in the know could find it. I can't imagine that much has changed."

Reese's mouth thinned. "How come no one has ever told us about this place?"

He knew, then. He knew about the hazing, the rituals, and maybe some problems that Mike hadn't even heard of.

"Beta Phi likes its secrets," Mike said. "Everyone swears a blood oath to keep certain rituals secret. Sometimes that includes the place where those rituals take place."

"What happens if you violate that oath?" Reese asked, peering at him, probably wondering why Mike was willing to do so.

Even if Mike cared about Beta Phi, which he no longer did, he would have violated that oath to keep Kizzie and Amanda safe. He had failed at keeping Amanda safe, but he could still protect Kizzie.

"Stuff that's not important when you reach my age," Mike said. "The Beta Phi members promised to block any career path, ruin someone's future, and destroy any chance that a former member had of complete success."

"Yet you kept the place secret," Reese said, as if the secrecy was Mike's fault.

"Not intentionally," Mike said. "I haven't thought of it in years, not until you mentioned the tower."

Reese turned away, spoke softly on his radio, and then sighed.

"They want you up there. They can't find any entrance to the basement or any evidence that the basement exists."

"Yet, I'll wager that Luke's phone is pinging from the tower itself," Mike said.

Reese frowned at him. "Yeah."

"He's there," Mike said. "I know it."

"He might have just left his phone behind," Reese said.

"Luke's not the brightest apple in the bunch when it comes to technology," Mike said. "Besides, he probably thinks he's safe in that basement. Probably figures he can lay low until you call off your search."

"How would he know when we do?" Reese asked.

"He has someone on the outside," Mike said. "Someone who's keeping an eye on you."

Maybe even the shooter. Mike shivered and glanced over at Kizzie. She was watching him from her chair inside the office. Her face was tear-streaked, her hands bunching the hem of her shirt, as if she didn't know what to do with them.

His gaze met hers and he willed her to get the message that he loved her and she was safe.

But she looked so lost.

"I need to talk to Kiz," he said.

"And then you're heading to the tower," Reese said.

Mike shook his head. "I'm sure you have access to the Beta Phis, maybe even have one on staff."

Reese let out a bitter laugh. "That fraternity? They loathe us. There has never been a Beta Phi in the police department and I doubt there ever will be."

Kizzie was leaning over the armrest now and Mike could sense what she wanted. He wasn't psychic. Anyone could figure this out.

She wanted him in the office.

"We need you, Mr. Cummings," Reese said. "That's the

fastest way to catch Mr. Brocado, if, indeed, he is where his phone says he is."

Mike looked at Reese, who had a steely expression on his face. Mike wasn't going to be able to argue this away.

"I need to talk to Kizzie first," Mike said. "That's non-negotiable."

"I would expect no less," Reese said, and then smiled. The smile was human, warm, and understanding.

It almost undid Mike, so he nodded and looked away.

Then he went to talk to the youngest victim of this entire mess, the child of his heart, the girl he thought of as his daughter, Kizzie.

His decision to talk to Kizzie nearly undid him. She crawled into his arms and sobbed.

"I can't reach Mom," she said, and he started when he heard that. "They won't give me my phone. Can I use yours?"

He kept his arms around her, and his back to the door. He could feel Reese's gaze on him, though, staring straight through, hurrying him along.

They did need to catch Luke so that Kizzie would feel safe. So that *Mike* would feel safe.

"I can't give you my phone, Kiz," he said. "I need it. I have—"

"Did *you* talk to Mom?" Kizzie asked.

He shook his head, then realized she couldn't see him.

"Not yet," he said. "I tried calling her earlier."

All true. He wasn't going to tell Kizzie about the deposition or about her mom's condition, not right away, not if he had to leave right now.

"So *call her*," Kizzie said, pulling out of his arms. Her expression was fierce, her face red from the tears and the anger and the sheer panic.

"I will," Mike said, "but first I have to go with the police."

"What?!" Kizzie asked. "They want to arrest you? I'll tell them, Mike, you're not doing anything wrong. I'll—"

She started to squirm off the chair as she said this, and he caught her arm.

"It's okay, Kiz," he said. "I'm going with them because they need my help. They're not going to arrest me."

She stopped, one foot flat on the floor, the other leg still curled on the chair's seat. Her hands clutched the armrest.

"I need you more," she said.

That was probably true. He sighed.

"I think I know where your dad is," he said.

"So *tell them*," she said, "and stay here with me."

"I did tell them," he said. "They can't figure it out."

She squinted at him. "How come you know and they don't?"

He had vowed, from the moment he saw her, that he would always tell her the truth. He wasn't going to stop now.

"It's a fraternity thing," Mike said. "It goes back to college."

She studied him. He always felt that, even when she was a baby, she had the ability to see right through him. He saw that in her eyes now. If he lied, she would see it.

He hated having to tell the truth. It was ugly today, and might get uglier.

"Can I come?" she asked.

"No," he said.

"Because it's not safe, right?" she asked. "Because you might get hurt too."

There was that, but he wasn't going to say it. He didn't dare worry her or let that thought go deep into his own head.

"I suppose there's a slim chance of that," he said. "But the police won't let you go. I know that for certain. They don't have the ability to watch you, and even if they did, they—and I—can't predict what your dad will do if he sees you."

Kizzie's face scrunched up in complete fury. "I *hate* him, Uncle Mike," she said. "I *hate* him. This is all his fault."

Mike didn't even try to jolly her out of the emotion. She was right, and the emotion was true and fair.

"It is," Mike said. "That's why the police are involved. They'll make him pay for what he's done. We just have to catch him first."

There was a knock on the door, and then it opened. Reese stuck his head in.

"Clock's ticking, Mr. Cummings," Reese said.

Mike put his arms around Kizzie, even though it was hard to do, given how she was sitting. He got a mixture of elbows and knees and one boney shoulder.

She put her arms around him, reluctantly, he thought, but as he was having that thought, she squeezed him tight. He squeezed her too, because he really didn't want to let her go.

He did though. He leaned back and stood up in the same move.

"I'll see you soon," he said.

"Make them give me my phone, Mike," she said, and he knew why. She wanted him to keep her apprised and she wanted to reach her mom.

"When I get back," he promised. "Just as soon as I get back."

They took him in the back of a squad car, as if he were one of the criminals—not that there was any room for him up front. Still, he didn't like the bench seat which felt a little crusty, despite the smell of cleaning fluid that permeated the squad.

Reese didn't drive him. Reese was staying at Harry S., apparently to coordinate things. Instead, he had two officers take Mike to Arch Hill.

The officers were a mismatch—the young driver,

Officer Gerhardt, who barely looked old enough to shave, and Officer O'Shea, whose leather skin and dark eyes more than made up for Gerhardt's baby face.

Gerhardt drove, though, with O'Shea in the passenger seat. She was the one who used the radio to update their status to the scene at the tower, as the squad pulled out of Harry S.'s parking lot.

The Educational Complex was only about a mile from the university as the crow flies, but the drive could take as long as half an hour, with traffic. Mike expected the longer drive; what he hadn't expected was Gerhardt's knowledge of the back streets.

It started from the moment they left Harry S. The squad lurched into action, speeding up as it went the back way down the hill, using a service road that was normally blocked off. The road was badly paved, so the squad created a lot of dust as it wove its way down. Gerhardt might have looked like he was brand-new, but he drove like a wannabe street racer, with a confidence that only came from experience.

The service road turned into another that went around the back of the university and opened onto Fraternity Row. From there, Gerhardt took an alley that led to Arch Hill.

The base of Arch Hill was blocked by even more squad cars and a couple of motorcycles. A uniformed officer was setting up actual barricades.

All of this, even though no one knew if Luke was here or if he had ditched his phone inside the tower.

Mike's stomach clenched. This day was filled with surprises for him, and he didn't like a single one of them.

Gerhardt took the traditional route up Arch Hill. It was impossible to drive all the way to the tower, so cars had to park on a turnout about a half mile down the hill.

From the turnout, there was a paved path littered with historical signs, talking about how Arch Hill had once been the center of the city, and how a person could still see the foundations of some of the buildings that had once littered the hillside.

Gerhardt pulled the squad onto the turnout where it joined some unmarked cars with their lights on, as well as one tactical van. The other squads all seemed to be below.

A handful of people in suits milled, looking at tablets. It took Mike a moment to realize they were using a drone to search the more overgrown parts of the hilltop before they went up.

Gerhardt put the squad in park, and got out in almost the same movement. He slammed the door, rocking the squad, and making Mike feel even more anxious than he was.

O'Shea got out as well and didn't say anything to Mike. For a brief moment, he thought they were going to leave him in the squad, but then she came to the back passenger door and opened it, her expression impassive.

"His phone hasn't moved," she said. "It is on, though. We have a warrant so that we can see who, if anyone, he's talking with."

Mike nodded. He cared less about the actual procedure part of everything than he did about getting to Luke. Luke's appearance at Harry S. was suspicious in and of itself. Tied with what happened at that deposition (and Mike's mind skittered away from the details right now), the appearance seemed even more suspicious.

When Mike thought of it, he felt an undercurrent of fury, one he did not dare tap.

He was here to show the police the hidden part of the tower, not to deal with Luke by himself.

"Okay," Mike said to O'Shea. "I can't really explain how to find the basement of the tower. I know you've all been searching."

Other officers and two men in tactical gear had gathered around O'Shea. Both tactical officers had their helmets on so tight that it pushed their chins upward and made their faces look slightly puffy. They held long guns of a type that Mike didn't recognize.

Of course, Mike didn't know any type of gun, so that was irrelevant. What was relevant was that the guns looked powerful and they clearly meant business.

The tactical officers had other weapons around their utility belts, and Mike purposely didn't look at those. He didn't want to focus on them.

"If Brocado's in that basement," one of the tactical officers said, "can he hear us outside?"

Mike frowned. He couldn't really remember. He looked

at the officer's vest. A last name was sewn onto the bullet-proof vest. Espinosa.

"I came up here as a frat boy late at night, leading a group of really drunk pledges," Mike said. "And even though we were trying to be quiet, there was no quiet at all."

He hoped the people around him understood—the laughter, the giggles, the drunken comments, the occasional spew of vomit.

"Then I came back up a few times to help the senior members of the frat set up for pledge night. We came up during the day, and we were fairly quiet. There was nothing around us."

He tilted his head slightly, trying to conjure that scene. He couldn't, not really. Not in enough detail to answer their question.

"So, I don't know. I doubt it. The tower is stone and the place where I think Luke is hiding is a partial cave, so maybe not..." Mike's mouth had gone dry. He should have brought water from his car, but he hadn't been thinking of himself all morning.

"Or maybe so," the second tactical officer said. His name, also sewn onto his vest, read Djimet.

"Or maybe so," Mike repeated in agreement.

Djimet looked at Espinosa. "We go in as quietly as we can, just in case."

Espinosa nodded. The other officers did as well.

"We're going to need a small team, as we explained,"

Djimet said. "Two of you will be in charge of Mr. Cummings—

As if Mike was some kind of criminal himself. He really didn't like how he was being treated, and he knew part of that was his fear and part of that was the legal training. He wanted respect from them, and right now, he was just a source that could be a lot of trouble.

"—and two of you will bring up the rear, looking for other problems. Espinosa and I will go first and clear the path as best we can."

Djimet started toward the paved path.

"Wait!" Mike said. "That's not how we get there."

Everyone in the entire group looked at him as if he had lost his mind.

"There's another way to the back." He wasn't sure if it was more efficient to take the second way, but he couldn't care about that. It was the only way he knew. "Follow me."

He pivoted and headed away from the tower.

"That's not how you get to the tower," Gerhardt said from the squad. "You're going away from it."

As if Mike didn't know that.

"Yeah," Mike said, dismissing Gerhardt with a single tone of voice. Gerhardt wasn't coming along. "I know."

Mike walked to the edge of the turnout. There, he stopped at a pile of rocks that acted almost like a berm. Beyond them was a tiny trail that looked like a goat path. It wound even farther away from the tower.

The officers all trooped along with him.

"This is the path," he said.

They peered at it as if he had lost his mind.

"Should we check it out with a drone first?" one of the officers asked. She was standing toward the back with a tablet in her hand.

"I would hope that you already had," Djimet said curtly. "You said the drone has flown over every single part of this hill."

"Yes, but—"

"No buts," he said. "The drone can fly ahead of us, see if anything or anyone is hiding along the way. Mr. Cummings, give us a sense of where this thing leads."

Mike took a deep breath, and swallowed hard. They asked for a sense. He could only give them a vague sense, but he'd do his best.

"It goes west, away from the tower, I think because that's a more solid path," he said. "Remember, the pledges come up here drunk and in the dark, so they need some solid footing."

"Then we should just take the regular path," said one of the officers behind Mike.

"No," Mike said. "This I know for sure. You can't get to the entrance from the main path."

He'd made that same complaint when he'd come up here in the daylight all those years ago, and had received the same answer he had just given the police.

"The path hits what feels like a ridge," he said, remembering how good that ridge had felt when he reached it, "and then it veers back toward the tower. It goes above the tower, and back when I walked it, there was a lot of undergrowth and brambles and such. You couldn't see the door with the naked eye."

"Is the door locked?" someone asked from behind him.

"Yeah," Mike said. "There's a key hidden near the base of the door. The key shouldn't be hard to find, but if they still keep it in a Beta Phi box, you'd need to know the Beta Phi house code."

"House code?" Djimet said. "Wouldn't they change it?"

"No," Mike said. "It's something in the pledge."

He sounded certain, but he really wasn't. He didn't know how kids did things now.

"You still know the code?" Djimet said.

"Memorized so thoroughly I could write it in my sleep," Mike said.

Djimet looked at the woman with the tablet, and said, "Unleash the drone. Stay in touch so that we know exactly what's going on."

"Will do," she said.

"All right, everyone," Djimet said. "Radios on. We're going up silently just in case this guy can hear us."

"I don't have a radio," Mike said.

"You don't need one," Djimet said. "Tap me on the back and point."

Great. How stupidly primitive.

Mike stared at those rocks and didn't look down at his feet although he wanted to. He was wearing his most comfortable dress shoes—a pair of loafers that he mostly lived in. And like the good professional that he was, he kept them polished, so that he looked like a man whose life was in order.

He was going to pay for that little bit of vanity now.

"Okay," he said. "It's up that way. I can go first." Because it would be easier than tapping and pointing. At least in his mind.

"No," Djimet said firmly.

He was the first to step over the rocks and to get onto the path. He held his long gun (rifle? Mike did not know) kitty-corner across his torso, and it looked like it would take very little for him to swing it out and put it to use.

Espinosa climbed over the rocks, and then Mike followed, focusing on his feet. He wasn't just wearing stupid shoes, he was also years out of shape. He couldn't remember the last time he had climbed a hill or done much running.

A trail that had seemed easy when he was twenty now looked daunting as hell.

The hard-packed brown dirt tilted inward on both sides, with a little line down the middle, almost as if water had created this path, not goats or frat boys. It probably would have been easy to traverse in boots or tennis shoes, but Mike's loafers didn't bend that way. He slid more than once, only to be propped up by an officer on the side.

Finally that officer whispered, "Look, walk the edge," breaking the silence to help Mike. Mike felt stupid as he climbed over to the looser dirt on the right of the path. He couldn't walk there entirely, but most of the way had loose dirt along the side.

The sun was beating down on them, and that dryness he had felt earlier was becoming an actual problem. Or maybe he wanted it to be, so that he could quit.

The path seemed longer than he remembered, and he was beginning to doubt himself when he saw the V-shaped turn that doubled back to the tower on a little ridge line.

Djimet stopped right there, looked over his shoulder, and inclined his head toward the tower, clearly asking *Is this it?*

Mike nodded, and Djimet turned, followed by Espinosa. Mike turned too, relieved that this part of the path was a little smoother. They all walked quickly, and as they did, Mike could hear some soft chatter from the headphones of one of the cops. There was something going on, or maybe not going on, or maybe they were getting a read from the drone.

Sweat ran down his back as the trail curved upwards. This looked unfamiliar. Someone had trimmed the overgrowth and planted some saplings. He wondered if the Beta Phis had done that so that the path would be even more hidden.

Although he thought that the presence of the trees made the path seem clearer, not more hidden.

Ahead, though, he saw the familiar overgrowth. No one

had messed with that, as far as he could see. No one had trimmed it back or even added to it.

What the growth was were blackberry brambles, tall grass, plants he didn't recognize, and a few bushes, struggling to survive. From a distance, it looked the same as always, massive and impenetrable. Up close, he knew there would be a way in, even if the entire group had to crouch.

When he'd come up here with Luke in the daylight all those years ago, Mike had remarked that the overgrowth and the little tiny entrance below looked like some kind of fantasy portal, maybe something out of Tolkien.

Luke had laughed and said, *More like* Monty Python and The Holy Grail. *That cave where the Black Beast of Aaaargh lives.* And then he had laughed again at Mike's confusion at the reference. *You know. The killer bunny.*

Ever after, Mike had thought that a small, cute, fluffy bunny with big, nasty teeth would fly out of the brambles and latch onto whomever went first.

He had that moment now, vaguely wondering if he had been sober when Luke had put that image in his head. There were no killer bunnies, but there might have been a killer.

His brain shied away from that. He had known Luke forever. He was not that kind of man—although Mike had had that very thought and felt it shatter just after Luke had backhanded Amanda across the mouth at the courthouse.

The two tactical officers had stopped, almost like they couldn't believe what was ahead.

Mike followed instructions and tapped Djimet on the arm, then as Djimet turned ever so slightly so that he could see Mike out his peripheral vision, Mike pointed.

"It's overgrown," Djimet said, using a soft voice to break the mandated silence.

"Not entirely," Mike said, just as softly. "It's designed that way to keep people out. Believe me, there's a path in."

Djimet didn't move for a moment, then shook his head. "I don't want you to go first," he said, almost as if Mike had argued for it.

Mike didn't want to go first either. "If it's like I remember," he said, "the growth isn't as formidable as it looks, and there's a place to gather near the door."

"If that's the door," Espinosa said, "it's not anywhere near the tower."

"Not the part you know," Mike said. "Remember. That used to be a huge building, and the tower was just one section."

They probably didn't know that. How many people read the historical markers, after all? How many knew the history of the places they lived?

"Command is saying it's close enough," one of the officers said quietly from behind. "And the ground does have a downhill slope that goes toward the tower itself."

Mike wasn't sure how the slope would make a difference, but he didn't say anything about that. Something about that information made the tactical officers move forward, though, and they crept along in what looked to him like an uncomfortable half crouch, something he couldn't have done for more than a few steps even when he had been young.

They moved with military precision, and Mike just walked, blisters forming on the side of his right foot as he tried to keep himself oriented on the trail.

They got through the trees which ended several yards from the overgrowth. Djimet stopped and Espinosa reached his side. Mike caught up with them a second or two later, trying not to limp.

His aching stomach flipped. He wasn't sure he would find anything here. Maybe the entrance had overgrown, and he was wrong.

But if he was, why then had Luke come here? To toss his phone? That would make no sense at all.

"I don't see an entrance," Djimet whispered.

Mike nodded and pushed past them. For a moment, he didn't see one either. The tangle was worse than he remembered, thick dark canes extending out from the ground near blackberry bushes, the thorns looking sharp and lethal up close. Some green plants, almost like grass, appeared below, and then there was the thick stump of an ancient tree.

It was the stump that jogged his memory. He crouched deeply, put a hand on the dirt in front of him and peered forward, until his eyes adjusted.

Then he saw it, the little hollow that the Beta Phis

maintained just past the stump. If anything, that hollow looked bigger than it used to.

"It's there," he said, and then looked at the brambles. That would be the tough part for him. The others wore uniforms or gear that protected them from the thorns. He didn't have anything on except a thin shirt and his least dressy pants.

For a moment, he toyed with staying behind, but there was one more hurdle for them to cross. The key. They needed it. The door to the basement was metal and it opened outward. They wouldn't be able to use force to break it open.

As he stood there indecisively, wondering if he could just tell them how to locate the key (if, indeed, it was in the same place), something hit his back. He turned.

The officer who had told him to walk up the trail on the side just put his jacket on Mike's shoulders.

The jacket was too warm and needed to be washed. It was too big as well.

"For the pickers," the officer said, thinking that was the entire reason for Mike's hesitation. The officer wasn't wrong. But Mike would be trapped in there with four people carrying guns and a man he had once thought he had known.

Then Mike saw Kizzie's devastated face, remembered how Amanda had looked after Luke had slapped her, and knew he had to do one more thing.

"Thank you," he said, and before anyone could argue

with him, he went forward, into the darkness, circling the base of that old stump to the trail that looked fresher than it should have.

It smelled of greenery and broken tree limbs, a touch of sap, and some crushed blackberries. The thorns brushed against his back, and some scratched his cheek. He had to go lower, which he did, crawling now, something he hadn't done in years—maybe since Kizzie was little and he was playing with her.

The distance from the stump to the hollow was farther than he expected, but someone had already pushed back most of the brambles. And they had carved out more room near the door, which surprised him. Before that area only fit about two people at a time. Now, he could stand there, and make room for the tactical officers scurrying behind him.

If they wanted silence, they were failing to achieve it. Their boots scratched against the ground and the brambles rustled. Even though no one spoke, it was clear that something—or someone—big was coming through the underbrush.

They arrived—Djimet first. He had thorns along one arm and some green leaves that might've been poison ivy sticking out of his tactical helmet. Mike resisted the urge to remove them. Instead, he pointed to them, and Djimet pulled them away, fortunately with a gloved hand.

Espinosa was right behind him. Both officers looked at Mike, not at the door.

He didn't blame them for missing it. It was covered with moldy green and black slime. The bottom of the door had rusted away, some leafy green vines were claiming the side of the structure. All of it had been built into the hillside.

Mike knew there was a hallway inside that led to the bottom of the tower, and a rung ladder that had rotted away before he had ever gone in this part of the building. That ladder probably led to a door, but one of the other frat guys had said that someone had put down a concrete floor, covering the entrance down here. Mike had never gone to check.

He started to grope for the flat stone with Beta Phi's symbol—its Greek letters, which looked kind of like a B—followed by a square with a line from the top of the square to the bottom, in a circle with spikes around the outside. He found the stone, then tossed it aside. There was no box in the little hole, and no key, either.

His stomach sank. He had led the police here, and they wouldn't be able to get in. Luke had taken the key.

Then he saw that the door looked slightly off. At first, he thought Luke hadn't closed it. Then he realized that one of the vines had slipped between the door and its frame near the top, maybe as Luke had gone in.

Mike turned and pointed upward.

Djimet frowned, then looked up. He grinned—not really anything with joy, but a gotcha-grin.

The officers were just pushing their way into the

hollow. Djimet pointed to one of them, and then at Mike. Djimet waggled his finger, a command to get Mike out of here, and the officer who had given Mike the jacket reached for Mike's arm.

Mike wanted to say, *You don't have to tell me twice* but didn't. Sound traveled through that metal hallway, and this group had probably made enough noise that Luke would be prepared for them.

Mike worked his way to the opening, and crawled into it, feeling the brambles against his back. He tried to bend down, but that didn't work, so he put his forearms down, getting through this part of the tunnel by using his elbows to pull himself forward.

He had to lower himself further near the stump. The group had clearly loosened some of the brambles. He could feel them in his hair. Some of the thorns scratched his skull, and a trickle of sweat ran down one side of his face.

He emerged into the bright sunshine and threw himself on the side of the trail. He wiped off the sweat, pulled his hand back, and realized that what he thought was sweat was actually blood from the thorns.

He hoped that would be the worst of it.

He peeled off the jacket and handed it to the officer, mouthing "Thank you" as he did so.

The officer nodded. His face was scratched and he looked stressed. He signaled to Mike that they had to move away from this entrance.

Mike stood, feeling awkward, his legs aching. The front

of his clothing was covered with dirt and leaves. He hadn't been this filthy in years.

The officer led Mike to the trees. They had just reached the edge when a gunshot sounded. Mike threw himself down, but the officers pivoted, guns drawn, pointing at the opening in the dirt.

"We need more people up here," said one of the officers into the radio pinned to his uniform. "Something's going on in that room."

"Get out of here," the second officer said to Mike, and he didn't have to be told twice.

He pushed himself up, then ran-walked along the trail, wishing he could just go straight down through the trees. He heard another gunshot, fainter this time. And then a third.

His heart was pounding, and he could barely keep himself moving. He'd never heard so many gunshots in his entire life—first at the law offices and now here.

He was sliding as he hurried, with nothing to grab onto if he fell. For the second time that day, he found himself going one way as other people went the other.

This time, the others were the police who had been on the turnout, running up to this site. They dodged him as if he were a boulder in their stream.

He slipped badly at the turn and bumped painfully halfway down the ridge on his butt. He didn't hear any more shots, but he heard a lot of yelling—faint, in the distance. Maybe he was too far away to hear gunshots.

He half-slid, half ran down the rest of the trail, using the rocks on the side to keep him as steady as he could be. Every few minutes, more officers ran up the trail as if it were nothing. None of them looked at him.

He finally reached the turnout. Gerhardt was near the squad and O'Shea was on her radio. Another tactical officer stood near their giant vehicle, and a single EMT stood near the small ambulance.

He came forward as Mike hit the turnout.

"There's shooting!" he said to Gerhardt and then realized how stupid that sounded. They were all in contact on the radio and probably knew more than he did.

Still, he couldn't stop himself from saying, "Someone's up there, probably Luke."

"It is Mr. Brocado," Gerhardt said. "They have him in custody now."

"Who got shot?" Mike asked.

"No one," Gerhardt said. "Mr. Brocado shot at them. He missed."

Gerhardt's voice was flat as he said that, but Mike heard so much more in those two words. *He missed.* Luke tried to shoot at the police, and he missed.

It must have been exceptionally loud in that cave/room. It had been loud in there with drunken pledges singing and puking and reciting the filthy poems they were assigned. Mike couldn't imagine what it actually sounded like in there with percussive gunshots in such close quarters.

Not to mention the bullets. Would they ping off the

walls? Or go through? There was no through in the cave part, and he wasn't sure if there was a through in the metal part either. The basement was underground after all, and on the other side of that metal there was either stone or dirt, he wasn't sure which.

"Mr. Cummings?" the EMT was beside him.

Mike started. He hadn't seen the EMT arrive. She was slight, with dark hair pulled back in a bun, and dark eyes that seemed to see everything.

"Let me get you cleaned up," she said. "I want to find out where that blood is coming from."

"Just thorns," he said.

"They can get infected," she said. "Come with me."

He let her lead him to the ambulance. He sat on the back, just inside the double doors, as she cleaned his face, traced the blood trail, and pulled a handful of thorns from his skull.

He focused on the radio dispatches and watched the trail. They had announced they had a prisoner, and they were coming down. There had been no announcement of injuries.

The EMT put a bandage beside his right eye. Mike hadn't even realized he'd been scratched there. She helped him clean off his hands and gave him a smock, taking his filthy shirt from him. ("It's covered with pickers," she said.) She didn't have anything for his legs, but she examined them to make sure there was nothing stuck in his skin.

He smelled of antiseptic, and parts of his face stung where she had cleaned him off.

Then she left out all of the cleaning tools, as well as a little bowl filled with thorns.

She smiled, maybe to herself. "I suppose I'm going to have a heck of a collection of those by day's end," she said, as if she weren't in the middle of the worst event that Mike had experienced in his life.

Maybe it wasn't the worst for her. Maybe she measured everything in casualties. Here, there wasn't going to be many, at least from the way she was acting.

The officers were finally trooping down the hill. Some immediately went to their vehicles and drove off, as if they had somewhere better to go. They probably did.

Others gathered around O'Shea. A few stepped to one side and spoke quietly into their radios. One got into a squad and sat, with the passenger door open, making notes on a computer. Another officer—the first's partner, maybe? —opened the back passenger door of the squad and appeared to be cleaning it out.

Finally the tactical officers came down the trail, Luke between them. His hands were cuffed behind him. He was as filthy as Mike—maybe filthier. Dirt was smeared across Luke's face so that only his blue eyes showed. They looked unfamiliar, dark, and glittery, not the warm laughing eyes that Mike used to associate with one of his closest college buddies.

The officers had to help Luke over the berm, and onto

the turnout. Their help was not kind. They picked him up by his arms and swung him forward, banging his shins against some rocks—probably deliberately.

Luke grunted, but didn't complain. Those blue eyes searched the turnout, and finally his gaze alighted on Mike, standing near the ambulance.

"You fucking bastard," Luke said. "You broke your oath."

Mike's mouth opened just a little. Luke's words felt like actual blows.

"You're not supposed to tell *anyone* about that basement. You pledged a blood oath."

"Mr. Brocado," Djimet said, shaking Luke a little, "you've been cautioned—"

"You bastard!" Luke said. "I thought you were my *brother.*"

Mike swallowed. The EMT put her hand on his arm, either to give him support or maybe hold him back if he charged forward.

Mike wasn't going to charge at all. Instead he felt rooted, as if he were attached to the ground.

He spoke before he even realized he meant to.

"I am *not* your brother," he said. "Gary's your brother, and…" Mike let his voice trail off. He didn't know what he was supposed to say, what Luke knew or didn't know.

"Gary was a bastard too," Luke said. "He kept telling me I had forfeited my rights."

Was. That was the word that echoed through Mike's

head. *Was.* Luke knew something, or maybe the officers had told him.

The officers, they were allowing this conversation to continue, not stopping Luke after that first lame attempt.

"Why weren't you at the deposition?" Mike asked, trying not to let this moment pass. If he could get Luke to hang himself, then it would be better for all.

"They told me that I was too volatile," Luke said. "Gary said he would handle it. Every time he's handled something, I've lost."

Mike was breathing through his mouth. His knees were a little weak. He didn't like what he was thinking.

"You didn't ask about Kizzie," he said.

"She's fine," Luke said. "I know she's fine. I was at the school until you showed up, you jerk. She's *my* daughter, not yours. I was going to take her with me when the news broke, but I knew—"

He stopped himself almost as if he realized what he was doing.

"What did you know, Luke?" Mike asked.

Luke's face scrunched into something vile, his eyes flashing, the expression so malevolent Mike would have taken a step back if there had been a step to take.

"That you wouldn't let me take her out of the school," Luke said. "That Amanda trusted *you*, even though you're not Kizzie's father, and that that horrid school believed *you* over me, and I didn't have time to argue. I got away. I got away, and I would've been fine if you hadn't broken your blood oath, you fucking traitor."

Mike parsed the sentences, and heard what was beneath. Luke had meant to take Kizzie...after the shooting at the deposition? Was Luke really behind it?

But Kizzie had thwarted him, not Mike, not that Mike was going to say anything. She saw Luke and called, and that plan went south. Police combed the area, and Luke tried to get away, but his car broke down. So he went to the only secret place he knew: the frat hideout on Arch Hill.

Knowing the plan made Mike feel worse. The chill around his heart seemed worse than ever. He had had no idea how truly depraved Luke was.

How had Mike missed that?

He straightened his spine, and said, "I didn't swear a blood oath, Luke." Mike's voice was calm. "I thought it was stupid. So I didn't violate anything, although I would have to keep you away from Kizzie."

"She's not your daughter!" Luke screamed.

"Biologically, no, she's not," Mike said. "But that's probably the only claim to fatherhood that you have, Luke. Your dick works."

Luke tried to shake off the officers and lunge for Mike, but they held Luke fast.

Djimet's gaze met Mike's. Djimet was covered in dirt too, but with his tactical gear, he looked like a man who had just come out of the jungle in some war movie.

Djimet raised his eyebrows ever so slightly and then

grinned. He was standing just outside of Luke's peripheral vision, so Luke missed it.

Then Djimet shook Luke and dragged him toward that open squad car door, shoving Luke into the back with very little ceremony. The officer near that squad closed the door, and got into the squad, as did another officer.

Together, they drove the squad to the other exit for the turnout, taking Luke out of the area.

Mike's knees collapsed. He landed on the edge of the ambulance, jolting his thighs and buttocks. He nearly slid off, but the EMT caught him. He was shaking.

He couldn't completely collapse. He couldn't quit. Kizzie was waiting for him, and he needed to know what was going on with Amanda.

Djimet walked over as Espinosa went to the tactical vehicle.

"Thank you," Djimet said.

Mike wasn't sure what Djimet was thanking him for. Obviously Mike looked confused, because Djimet added, "We wouldn't have found him without you."

Mike let out a breath. One step completed then.

"Was anyone injured?" Mike asked.

"No," Djimet said. "He heard us and fired a warning shot, then fired when we went in. He clearly had had no firearms training. Despite the location, it was an easy arrest."

Mike had been practicing law long enough to know that an arrest did not a case make.

"Now what?" he asked.

"That's not up to me," Djimet said. "There will be an investigation. You pulled some information from him, so that was helpful."

"If you really did caution him before I saw him," Mike said. He hadn't heard any do-not-talk warning from the police.

"We did," Djimet said.

"Then it's admissible." Mike probably didn't have to explain that, but it was good to say it anyway.

"Yep," Djimet said, "for a lawyer, he's not the brightest bulb in the chandelier."

Mike smiled. Luke used to say the same thing about Gary.

Then Mike's smile faded. He had no idea if Gary was alive. So much had happened this morning that this was not really the end of anything. Just the beginning of the aftermath.

"Just wanted to say thanks," Djimet said, and headed to the tactical vehicle.

The EMT handed Mike a bottle of vitamin water, which he downed. It gave him a moment to recover, and just a little more energy.

He would need it.

He had no idea what else this day would require of him.

G erhardt and O'Shea drove him back to the school. They didn't say much, but the radio chattered with codes that revealed just a bit of the investigation.

Luke had not been the shooter at the law office—obviously. He couldn't have driven there and back. But it sounded like someone was on the shooter's trail, and some of the voices that came through the radio sounded...not excited but not calm either.

Mike leaned his head back, but not before noting that Gerhardt had driven the usual roads to get to Harry S., not the back roads. The police presence was gone at the base of the hill.

Apparently, Harry S. was no longer under immediate lockdown.

Kizzie was probably going nuts without him there, and he was going to show up in a smock and mud-covered pants. He had one bandage near his eye, and he probably looked really banged up.

He had no idea what he would say to her.

The squad turned up the familiar winding road to the Educational Complex. There were a lot more cars in the parking lot at Harry S. Some probably belonged to parents. Others were clearly police-issue.

"Do you know what exactly happened at the law office?" he asked O'Shea because he couldn't wait any longer. "Did everyone make it out alive?"

He knew the answer even before she turned around and gave him a compassionate look. He almost didn't see her movement as his mind revisited that scene: the man—Gary?—on the floor, his face pressed into the blood; the woman face down on the conference table, arms splayed; the whimpering.

He might never forget the whimpering.

"Two died," O'Shea said quietly. "I think you probably know one of them."

His stomach clenched again. He hadn't thought it could recede farther into itself this day, but it was trying. His heart, which had ached all morning, was starting to beat faster.

Maybe Amanda hadn't made it. Maybe she had died in the hospital. Maybe he had been wrong not to take Kizzie there immediately.

"Mr. Brocado is one of the victims," O'Shea was saying. "Luke Brocado's brother."

Mike had known it. He had known it from the moment he had seen the body.

"And...?" he asked, fearing the answer. It felt like he had been gone for hours. That was more than enough time for Amanda to die in surgery.

"We're notifying next of kin now," O'Shea said.

"Lawyer? Court reporter? Legal Assistant? Person being deposed?" But he knew the answer to that last one even before he said it. The person being deposed had been Amanda.

"All of them were shot," O'Shea said gently. "Only the court reporter didn't make it out."

And Mike didn't know her. He assumed that was the woman sprawled over the table, but then he frowned. He'd run dozens of depositions. The court reporter always sat in a corner, typing quietly away.

So the woman sprawled over the table had been someone else.

He probably hadn't even seen the court reporter. She had probably fallen in her corner, a victim of being in the wrong place at the wrong time.

He was shaking. He didn't know how to do this.

"I've got to see Kizzie," he said, "and look at me."

"I'm sure she's probably not concerned that you're dressed up," O'Shea said.

He had initially thought the woman hard, but she had a softness now as she spoke to him. She almost seemed concerned. Because he had helped catch Luke? Because this part was probably over?

"What do I tell her?" Mike asked. "Her father knew. He knew this was going down, and he was trying to kidnap her."

"Yes," O'Shea said, returning to the blunt woman she had been when Mike met her.

"He probably knew the killer," Mike said.

"Or hired him," O'Shea said. "That's the theory we're working on now, and there's evidence of it."

"But to shoot Gary…" Mike said. "Why would he do that?"

"I don't think it was intentional," O'Shea said. "What

we're getting from the scene—and realize this could change—is that Gary Brocado tried to stop the shooter and paid for that with his life."

Gary. The loser younger brother. The one Luke always made fun of. The one that Luke had had to settle for when everything fell apart.

Who knew that Gary was the stand-up person in that two-person family?

Gary might be the only reason Amanda was alive.

The squad pulled up to the main door. Mike wasn't quite ready to leave yet.

"Any word on Amanda?" he asked.

"Nothing specific," O'Shea said, "but in this case, for us, no news is good news."

Then she got out of the squad. Mike barely had a moment to gather before she pulled the side door open.

He got out, shaking just a little, wishing he could go home and change, knowing that everything was different. He was going to have to take Kizzie to his place, and then he was going to have to find out what was going on with Amanda.

He was going to convince her to go to North Dakota, when this was all over, to get away from here and start over so that Kizzie wasn't the kid whose Dad hired someone to kill her mother and managed to slaughter his uncle.

O'Shea reached a hand to him, as if she were the prince at a ball and he was the princess, getting out of the carriage. The image was so stark and different from what he was actually experiencing that he almost let out a laugh.

There was hysteria lurking behind that laugh, and he didn't dare let it out. In a few minutes, he was going to have to be the grown-up in the room.

Mike took O'Shea's hand and let her help him out of the squad. He staggered just a little—his legs were still wobbly—and then he stood. O'Shea didn't let go of his fingers, not yet.

"That little girl in there?" O'Shea said. "She's lucky to have you."

Mike hadn't expected that from O'Shea. He hadn't expected anyone to notice him, not really. He was the guy who was always there, but never appreciated. Except by Kizzie.

Only now, O'Shea saw him too.

"Thank you," he said, hoping she understood that his reaction was heartfelt and not perfunctory.

Then he let her hand go and walked to the front of Harry S. Someone opened the airlock for him—he didn't see who—and he stepped farther in, noting a police officer, some people in the hallway, lots of chatter.

Apparently, some parents wouldn't leave, even though the school had decided to continue classes. The assistant principal, a young man whom Mike had talked to a few times, was gesturing and making a point, when he stopped and looked over his shoulder at Mike.

The parents did too.

Mike thought of saying something flip, but he wasn't feeling flip. He nodded at them and went to the principal's office.

Kizzie was standing near the glass door, next to Zander, who had a hand on her shoulder. Two parents were in Principal Hallenbeck's office with her, and the door was closed, even though the shouting was clear from here.

"Mike!" Kizzie said when she saw him. She ran toward him, then skidded to a stop. "Can I hug you?"

He did look bad if a little girl could see it and be solicitous of it.

"Please," he said, and she completed her launch, hitting him so hard that he staggered backwards.

Zander's hand caught him. A lot of people were catching Mike today, and he didn't mind.

He held Kizzie so close, so very close. He wasn't ever going to let her go.

She was the reason that Luke got caught, the reason things didn't tip farther into horror. She had called Mike and Mike had come and Luke had run.

Mike wasn't sure how to tell her that. Nor was he sure what to say about her mother. There was going to be hospitals and decisions and probably therapists in all of their futures, not counting court cases and...

His brain shut down. He couldn't think about that right now.

"Let's go home," he said to Kizzie.

"I gotta see Mom," she said into his side.

"I know," he said. "Let me get changed first, and now you're covered in mud too."

"Where's that from?" Kizzie asked. She pulled back just a little.

"It's a long story," Mike said, "and I don't know all of it yet. So let's do this one step at a time. Home, change, hospital."

"That's three steps," she said, his anal girl, so like him. She was looking at his face, assessing what she saw there.

He had no idea what it was, but it couldn't have been reassuring.

"Yes," he said, knowing how to complete this circle. "That's three steps. We'll do them in order, okay?"

"Okay," she said. Then she stepped back and slipped her hand in his.

"I'm taking her out of here," he said to Zander.

Zander gave him a sad smile. "I expected no less."

Then he mouthed, *Good luck*. Mike nodded.

He already had the good luck. He'd gotten to Luke before this entire crazy scheme played out. Otherwise, Luke and Kizzie might've been heading who knew where, and the police would have been searching for Luke as next of kin, rather than as an accused criminal who had just kidnapped his daughter.

Mike had to focus too, just like he had told Kizzie to do.

One step at a time.

That was how they would get to their new future.

One step at a time.

BUT WAIT, THERE'S MORE!

Want more masterful mysteries?

Go to wmgbooks.com!

Sign up for the Kristine Kathryn Rusch newsletter, and keep up with the latest news, releases and so much more— even the occasional giveaway.

To sign up go to kriswrites.com

Get the latest news and releases from all of WMG's authors and lines, including Kristine Grayson, Kris Nelscott, *Pulphouse Magazine,* and so much more…

To sign up, **go to wmgbooks.com.**

ABOUT THE AUTHOR
KRISTINE KATHRYN RUSCH

Kristine Kathryn Rusch sold more than 35 million books worldwide. She publishes bestselling science fiction and fantasy, award-winning mysteries, acclaimed mainstream fiction, controversial nonfiction, and the occasional romance.

Her novels made bestseller lists around the world and her short fiction appeared in more than twenty best-of-the-year collections. She won more than twenty-five awards for her fiction, including the Hugo, *Le Prix Imaginales,* the *Asimov's* Readers Choice award, and the *Ellery Queen Mystery Magazine* Readers Choice Award.

To find out more about her work, go to her website, kriswrites.com

    facebook.com/kristinekathrynruschwriter
    patreon.com/kristinekathrynrusch
    bookbub.com/authors/kristine-kathryn-rusch

www.ingramcontent.com/pod-product-compliance
Lightning Source LLC
Chambersburg PA
CBHW030211130726
47898CB00012B/981